The Coma Monologues

Also by Mario Milosevic

Novels
Claypot Dreamstance
The Doctor and the Clown
Kyle's War
The Last Giant
Splitting
Terrastina and Mazolli

Collections
15 Strange Tales of Crime and Mystery
Entangled Realities (with Kim Antieau)
Labor Days
Miniatures

Poetry
Animal Life
Fantasy Life
Love Life

The Coma Monologues

Mario Milosevic

The Coma Monologues
by Mario Milosevic

ISBN: 978-1-949644-41-8

Cover image copyright © Alexei Sysoev | Dreamstime.com

Special thanks to Nancy Milosevic and Lucia Ploskey.

Electronic editions of this book are available at most ebook stores.

Published by Green Snake Publishing
www.greensnakepublishing.com

mariowrites.com

contents

christopher pratt

Hey, man.

[long pause]

That really you?

[coughs]

You look different. Gary Hawken. Man. Just your name takes me back.

[another pause]

[more coughing and a pronounced clearing of the throat]

Melody's got it in her head that you would want me to be first. I don't get it, but here I am. I made it. I couldn't get a direct flight from Las Vegas to Toronto. They were all booked up. I had to switch planes in Chicago. Pain in the ass, let me tell you. I hate flying anyway. Plus, now I gotta have a passport to get back into Canada. Or get back to the States. Whatever. Either way, it's a royal pain. Fucking terrorists. Ruined everything. Also, since I haven't been back here for ten years, maybe more, I forgot how fucking *cold* it is. And we're in March. Time for spring, you know? Hello, spring. We're fucking ready for you. Wake up! Let's stop sawing wood and get out here, okay?

Well, whatever. I'm supposed to tell you stories or something. You don't want to hear about the weather. Or maybe you do. Who the fuck knows? Not your doctor, let me tell you. Doctor Ayles. Cold fish, that guy. No bedside manner at all. That I can see. Doesn't know anything about what's going to happen to you. No one knows. Maybe you do. Or maybe you don't. Maybe you don't know anything. Do you even know who Melody is? Your wife, that's who. What the fuck is going on in that head of yours, anyway?

Your wife's an English professor. Remember that? Teaches college kids all about stories and shit. Literature. Maybe that's why she thinks stories can save your fucking life. Who the fuck knows? Maybe she's right.

They tell me you're still in there, locked up in your cranial capacity or something. Is it possible? I guess so. The nurse showed me this newspaper clipping about a guy who was in a coma for twenty-three years and then one day he woke up. Twenty-three years. Makes you think, that's for sure. How long has it been for you? Not even twenty-three days yet. You're just a kid at this. Man, I wouldn't want to be in your situation for twenty-three *minutes*. The doc says you only got about three months. If you don't wake up after that, well, chances are you ain't gonna. Forget about that twenty-three year guy. He's just a glitch. Oh. The nurses are back.

[pauses]

Well. Looks like there's a lot of maintenance to do on you everyday, with all the tubes and fluids and what not. Swapping out bags of— food—I guess. Water. Fucking *nutrients* or some such shit. Moving you around so you don't get bedsores. Draining your piss. Shit like that.

Don't worry though, they all look like they want to keep doing it. They're like robots or zombies or something. Intent on their duty. Oops. Maybe I shouldn't talk about zombies. Not that you're a zombie. That's not what I mean. Okay, forget all that. Just think about the nurses. Yeah, some of them are nice to look at. I appreciate a hot nurse as much as the next guy, know what I mean? But some of these nurses are guys themselves, so what can I say? The main thing is that they're all dedicated to keeping you going, okay? That must make you feel good. They want you back. It's kind of sweet. Here you are a lump of nothing, and they just want you back in the world. Shit. I didn't mean you're nothing. Forget that. You're something, okay? There's a great big one out here, buddy. A world, I mean. *The* world. You know? Don't you want to come see it? Don't you want to wake up?

[pauses]

Is this really doing anything? Or am I wasting my time here? I don't like leaving Vegas. It's my home. I'm getting so I resent ever going somewhere else. A town like Las Vegas, you have that in your life, you don't need anything else. It's got it all.

[pauses]

I've never seen anyone so white. It's like you're made of bread. All puffy like. But healthy! You know. Real healthy.

Oh, shit. I didn't tell you who I am. Chris. Remember me? We went to high school together. We were crazy for science fiction back than. Swapped paperbacks about aliens and space travel shit like other kids swapped baseball cards. Coupla first class nerds as I recall. Then I discovered girls. One in particular. You remember Lisa, right? Sweet girl. Built like a you know what. Shit. I *still* have dreams about Lisa. You never forget your first one, you know. It's true. I never forgot. Fucking twenty-five years later and I've still got a bone on for her. Wonder what happened to her. I guess I could find out, but maybe I want my memories more. Still, I wouldn't mind getting back with her, you know? Not a long term thing, or anything. I'm not made that way. Just for a night or two. A good time. Um, maybe I'm not supposed to talk about that kind of thing? I don't know. What the fuck. I wonder, can you, you know, get it up in your condition? Is it like a morning hardon? It just pops up? That'd be weird. Not that I'm so interested I want to see it or anything. Just idle curiosity is all. Probably they pump you full of something so that it doesn't happen. Or maybe they don't? Like who would care if you did? It'd just go down after a while, right?

Damn. Get me off this train of thought. It's not healthy for either of us. Anyway, if I remember from back then, it's not like you cared much. About girls, I mean. You mostly stayed away from them. Liked your books more, I guess. Not knocking it. Whatever works, right? We're all different. But anyway, me and you, we were friendly and everything after I developed my new interest, but we weren't really friends anymore. We'd say hi, and that's about it. You went to your chess tournaments and did your homework. I went to a lot of parties and learned other things. Remember any of that? My yammering on like this doing anything for you? After high school we didn't much know each other. You went to university. Some fancy ass school to learn engineering. Figured you'd improve your life or something. Hah! That didn't work out the way you planned, did it? I mean, considering your current predicament. Not that going to school had anything to do with your coma. I'm just saying life is funny what it does to you.

Me. I was never cut out for school. My parents gave me a hard time about it, telling me to at least try it for a year. A semester. Whatever. But we are what we are, right? I couldn't see sitting in classrooms for four years. God, I would die. By my own hand. Put a gun to my head and end it all with one pull of the trigger if anyone made me study for fucking *years*. I went to work for a garage for a while after high school. I was pretty good at cars and engines and shit. But that didn't last. I was too young to be stuck in a stupid job. So I went traveling. Saw a bunch of the world. You know what I discovered? In foreign countries *I* was the exotic foreigner. Wow. I didn't have to do much pursuing, I'll tell you that. Women flocked to me, and I'm not kidding. Not lying, either. You can believe it or not. It's the truth. Eventually I got to playing cards and got pretty good at it. Now I drive a limo in Vegas and gamble my tips. Not my fares. That's for paying bills and saving. I'm responsible, you know. I have a house, pay a mortgage. Women like a guy with a nice house. But my tips? That's a different story. I take that money and go to the poker tables. That's how I financed the pool at my house. And my big ass flat screen TV. Not to mention my car. Other shit, too. It's a pretty good life. Some casinos don't let me in anymore. They think I cheat. I don't. I'm just good at cards. Fortunately, Vegas has more casinos than I could ever gamble at in a lifetime.

Never got married or anything. No kids. Not that I know of, anyway. You've got a nice family. Your wife, she's pretty upset about all this. She's also kinda hot. Yeah, wouldn't mind spending some quality time with *her*. I think she'd want to do it with me. I felt this kind of spark between us, you know. The way she looked me over when I got to the hospital. It was nice. Made me feel warm inside, I'll tell you. Probably after I talk to you, me and her will find an empty room down the hall or something and get to know each other real well.

[pauses]

Sorry about that. I just wanted to see if you'd get steamed and wake up from your coma. No dice. But it was worth a try. Hope I didn't make you blow a gasket or anything. Forget all that what I said about your wife and me. There's nothing there. She's still in major grief about you. So really, don't worry; I wouldn't go after her or anything. I'm not that kind of guy. I never knowingly chase married women, never have and never will, and that's the honest truth. She's crazy about you. That's obvious to anyone. Found my name in your high school yearbook. Said I wrote: *keep reaching for the stars, dude.* I didn't remember that. Hell, I didn't remember we *had* a fucking yearbook. She figured I must have been some kind of friend of yours so she tracked me down on the internet. Shit, anyone can find anyone now, you know? She found some articles that said voices from the past can bring people back. So here I am. A voice from your past. Hello! Anyone in there?

[knocks edge of bed]

[laughs nervously]

[pauses]

I tell you, I don't think I'm much good at this. They tell me you need voices you recognize. That's supposed to bring you back. Stories, too. I'm supposed to tell you stories. Like I'm some kind of writer or something. I don't know any stories. Mostly they want me to keep talking talking talking.

[pauses]

I sound like an idiot.

[pauses]

To myself. Maybe to you, too. I don't know.

[pauses]

They told me what happened to you. You're driving along and some asshole truck driver runs a red light and smashes into you. Banged your head up pretty good. Good enough that you're in this fucking coma. Scary shit, man. I don't know what I would want if I was in your position. To keep going, or just fold my cards. Just say, okay, I've had my time. A pretty good run, but it's over. I'm not going to go on as a carrot lying on a hospital bed for a couple of decades. That's too hard on everyone. Maybe dying would be better. I'm just saying I would think about it. I would. If I could think anymore. That guy that went twenty-three years? He could hear stuff all that time. He took it all in. Spooky. Couldn't move a muscle, just like you. Couldn't do *anything* except listen. I'd go crazy, I think. I'd want to die after a few years of that. After a few *days* of that. Who wouldn't? You, maybe. I don't know. Do you want to die? You can't tell us, so we assume you want to live and we'll try to keep you alive. That's what people do, you know. They look after their kind. When they're not killing each other, which I noticed, people can be pretty good at. Look, they told me to avoid the topic of death, but fuck 'em. I'm supposed to talk to you one on one, okay? So I'm sure if you can hear anything, if you're still buried inside there somewhere, you've thought about death. Hell, you can practically touch the robes of the grim fucking reaper right now. Borrow his goddamn scythe for a shave. It's like you and he are neighbors. Am I right? Sure. Maybe you've got this white light all around you anyway, and you can't hear a thing cuz the light drowns everything out. Or maybe I'm like this unintelligible sound. Whaw whaw whaw. Like the teachers on the Charlie Brown shows. You liked those, didn't you? The whaw whaw whaw. I know you used to make that noise when you thought someone was an asshole. Oops. I was supposed to avoid profanity, too. Some people, when they're in comas, profanity really embarrasses them and they want to stay in the coma. That's what the nurses told me. Did you know that? Crazy, huh? Try to figure people. It's impossible. People in your situation create quite a quandary for the medical professions. They don't know what to do with you so they try crazy things. Like this. Like some guy from your high school days that you probably forgot about years ago, coming and talking to you. But I remember you weren't too bothered by profanity. Used it every chance you could get, from when we were kids. Remember how we knew all the curse words even when we were real young and we thought they were words kids made up? How crazy was that? I remember how we thought it was weird when we heard adults using our words. Fuck. We really were fucking nerds. Glad we grew out of it. Sure, nerds run the world, inventing things and making it all work, but they don't get any, is what I'm saying. But, hell, maybe you didn't grow out of it. Maybe you're still a nerd?

[pauses]

Do you even know who you are anymore?

[pauses]

Do you know *where* you are? You're in some hospital in Toronto. We grew up in Sudbury. Mining town. Smelters. Big smokestacks spewing shit into the air. Any of this ringing a bell? We went to Barrydowne High School. We worked at the Loblaw's store, bagging groceries and stocking shelves after school and on the weekends. Every time you saw the boss you made that whaw whaw whaw noise. Yeah, he was an asshole. Not his fault. It was his calling, I think. You went to University of Waterloo. You remember any of this? Any of your life?

[pauses]

Why do I keep asking you questions? I must be dumber than a post. There was this other guy I heard about. He was completely paralyzed. His whole body, except for two things. Can you guess? Go ahead and try. I'll give you time. I know you can't answer me, but you might be hearing me and thinking about it, so I'll give you a few seconds. It's like you'll never believe it. It's the weirdest thing.

[pauses]

Okay I'll tell you. His fucking eyelids! Can you believe it? The only thing on his whole body that worked were his eyelids. He couldn't even move his eyes. But he could hear and he could still think, so they figured out a kind of Morse code thing where he could communicate with his goddamn *eyelids*, blinking them open and closed. First message he blinked out was: *Please kill me.* I'm not kidding. He wanted to die. But they didn't kill him. We don't do that unless we have guns and the other guy is in a uniform. Then it's okay. *Then* it's fucking heroic, right? But to bring peace to someone by ending their wretched life? That's different. You wouldn't want to ever do something like that. Shit, no. Maybe for a *dog*, but not a human being. That'd be wrong.

[pauses]

So they persuaded him that even all gimped up like he was, I mean, gimped to the fucking *max*, he still had a life. Must have had some super goddamn powers of persuasion there, let me tell you. Eventually he blinked out something like: *Thank you for saving my life.* Kind of sad, really. But still. Wow. The whole eyelid thing. Communicating that way.

Did you guess it was the eyelids? I bet you did. You were always good at puzzles and stuff. Games. Riddles. You loved that shit. I could take it or leave it, but it was pretty cool how you seemed to enjoy it so much. You always beat me at chess. Too bad your eyelids didn't work. We could play a few games. You could blink out the codes for the moves. That would probably perk you right up. Maybe wake you up. Hey, that's an idea. I could play over some games for you. Would you like that?

[pauses]

I'm such an idiot, still thinking you can answer me. But it isn't my fault. You just look like you're asleep. You look like if I just kicked your foot you'd pop up in bed, wondering who the asshole is who kicked your foot. Me. I'm the asshole.

[pauses]

You got two kids. That's cool. I haven't met them. Still pretty young for all of this. What are they? Twelve and fourteen, right? A girl and a boy. Matched set. No reason to have any more if you got one of each, right? I wonder if they're going to have your kids come in and talk to you. Naw, that wouldn't be right. Be too traumatizing for them.

Some of the women I'm with, they want children. Not with me. Hell, no. I'm just a convenient fuck for them. Not that I'm complaining. That's all I ever want to be. But they talk to me about their lives. Almost all of them, if the subject comes up, they say they want children. Ache for them, you know. For women, it's not like they have to decide if they want children or not. They want them. They do. With guys, we got this thing going on in our heads: do I want to have kids or don't I? And we, like, make a conscious decision about it, one way or the other. Usually the other. But for women it's different. Their biology, I guess. I don't know. It's like they have to make themselves *not* want children, and it ain't easy for them. Is that what it was like with you and your wife? She have to talk you into it? Bet she did. Or maybe not. I don't know. Sometimes I wonder what it would have been like, you know, to have children. Anyway, maybe I fucking did, who knows? Maybe next week some teenager from fucking *Spain*, where I spent a few months, is going to knock on my door and say: *Hi Dad! Where you been all my life? Mom says I can get some money from you.* In fucking Spanish.

I'm prepared for it. I have some put away. The courts, you know, they'll make you pay for that mistake. Even if the mother kept the kid from you all that time, it doesn't matter. So it's good to have some insurance. They can prove shit now, too, with DNA and all that.

Not that I have anything against children. Sometimes people bring their little kids into the casino. Get them started early with gambling, I guess, who the fuck knows. But casinos are not for children. So they have to get escorted out. Sometimes there's a big scene, you know, people claiming harassment. Screaming about this is supposed to be a free country. Blah blah blah. Whaw whaw whaw. Let me tell you, there ain't no free country anywhere. Nothing's free. We all have to pay in one way or another. Or someone pays for you. Point is, there's a cost for everything. That's all I'm saying. But I sit at the poker table and take it all in, the drama. The fucking parade of humanity, you know? What I'm getting at is the kids, they're caught in the middle of the mess. They see all the lights and the excitement and shit. They think they're in Disneyland or something, but then their parents get them into a scene and you can see on their faces how it hurts them. I don't know. I'm just saying, a lot of people, they don't know how to take care of kids. Kids need some protection in life. A lot of protection. There's a lot of stuff that can hurt them. After they get to be a little older, then okay, it's time to toughen them up. Put them out in the world, you know? Sink or swim time. But you have to have this period of time when they got life preservers. That's all I'm saying. So maybe your kids shouldn't come in here and talk to you. Might be too much like being in the deep end of the pool.

[pauses]

I just thought of something. Right now, in your condition, you'd be a good poker player. You don't have any tells. Hah! Yeah, bad joke. So sue me. Really, though, I don't think you'd be a good poker player. You're good at games of skill. Where all the rules are laid out and everything. But poker isn't like that. Rules is like about five percent of it. Most of poker is psychological. You got to size up people and understand how they think. There's a big psychological element to it. You probably never chased women, so you never learned psychology. Not like you learn when you want to get into their panties. There's a world of education right there, let me tell you. A lot of psychology involved. That all transfers to the poker playing. Like, women got these tells. I can figure out in about thirty seconds if a woman can be persuaded or not. Sometimes I don't even know how I know it, but it's there. If I don't feel it within half a minute, I throw her back in the sea. But if I *do* feel it, well, I turn on the charm, you know. I ante up. I'm in the game for the long haul. And I usually get what I want.

They usually get what they want, too, so it's not like it's a one way street. Put it this way: I don't get any complaints.

[pauses]

Shit. Here I am talking to a family guy about my swinging single life. They taping this? Oh, shit. I didn't think of that. They didn't say they were going to. I don't see a recorder or anything. Maybe it's in the walls? Damn. They could have it anywhere. I better clean up my act. Get on the straight and narrow.

[pauses]

Well, I looked around the whole room and I don't think there's anything recording this. Maybe they should. After I'm gone they could play it over and over again for you. Yeah. Chris's philosophy of life put down for the ages. Hah!

[pauses]

Look, the thing is, you got a nice family. They want you back. So come back, okay?

[pauses]

Your wife tells me you design roads and shit like that. Highway overpasses. Work for the government, right? That's cool. All that stuff's gotta be built by someone. You're one of those someones. A nerd. You ever drive on the stuff you designed? Bet you do. That must make you feel good. Like you accomplished some important stuff. Don't you want to come back to design more overpasses? Maybe you could design like, a bridge, or something. How about a bridge across Lake Ontario? That'd be some kind of big project. You should come back and do that.

[pauses]

It's not supposed to be like this, man. Remember when we used to read that science fiction shit? We thought by now we'd have the jet packs and personal space ships and stuff. We'd zip up to the moon for the weekend, bounce around in the craters and shit. We'd take these goddamn pills and we'd live forever and be like twenty years old for twelve centuries or something. We really were the sorriest ass kids, swallowing all that bullshit like it was good for us. If any of that shit was true, or could be true, you wouldn't be like this now. Fucking future technology would make it so the doctors would just tweak this and poke that, flick a switch and inject some nano beasts into you that would swarm over your brain and pull and tug on the fucking neurons till they got you into a state where you'd wake up like you had just been taking a nap. But that's not what fucking happened, in case you didn't notice. Now you're a vegetable and *no one knows what to do about it.*

[pauses]

But okay. No one ever promised that the fairy tales from your childhood would come true. Or if they did, then they were practicing some kind of child abuse. My opinion, is all it is. Take it or leave it.

[pauses]

Well, I've had enough of this. You ever do wake up, come down to Vegas. I'll give you a free limo ride from the airport. Bring your family. Just remember, I came up here for you. I didn't have to. Who are you to me? Let's be honest. No one, that's who. But your wife sounded so scared on the phone. She needed help and she said I could help, so I came, okay? I'm a decent guy, really. I chase women, and I gamble some, but that's it. That's not so bad, you know. I could be doing a lot worse things.

I don't have a respectable life like you do, but I'm not a bad guy. I'm not. At my heart, I look after people too, when asked. I don't get asked much. Where I live, it can be lonely and people don't know how to be human sometimes, but that's not the whole thing. Sometimes they are really decent. Like me. I did the right thing. I tried to help out, okay? Remember that when you wake up. Not that you'll owe me or anything.

[pauses]

That's not what I'm saying.

[pauses]

Hell. Forget all that. You don't have to remember me. Just wake up. There's people here that miss you. Not me. Hah! Before last week, I hadn't given you two thoughts since high school. I'm talking about other people. They love you man, so ante up and get into the game.

Play your damn cards.

That's all.

isaac asimov

When I was still alive and had my apartment in Manhattan, my phone number was listed in the phone book. Even though I had some small measure of fame, I never saw any reason to keep my phone number a secret. I received phone calls from fans, and they were almost invariably pleasant conversations. I never forgot that the science fiction fans were the people who started me on my path to being a professional full-time writer.

As I recall, one of those phone calls came from you. I remember it quite vividly. Janet picked it up and said it was for me. I was in the middle of watching *Laverne and Shirley*, my favorite TV show, which I never missed, but I took the call anyway. You were quite nervous, which didn't surprise me. A lot of the people who called me were nervous. They were awed by me. I'm not boasting. I was famous for my immodesty, but modesty had nothing to do with it. I'm reporting a simple fact: when I walked the earth, there were many people who thought of me as some kind of genius. I knew better, but I never tried to dissuade them from that perception. It was no business of mine what people thought of me, and anyway, I liked being thought of in that way. Who wouldn't?

In any case, you were not like many of my callers who used me for quick answers to some of their science questions. Not just young people, but other professional writers would call me up willy nilly, needing the answers to some esoteric bit of information for their stories to make them more believable. Believability was important. Sure, we imagined future societies and marvelous new technologies, and we concocted fantastic inventions and spectacular spacecraft and so on, but it was always important to ground our flights of imagination in facts. Solid knowledge. And more often that not, I was able to assist them. It helped my reputation immensely, let me tell you. I became known as the font of all knowledge. Not just science, but other disciplines as well. Shakespeare, for example. And American history. Mythology. I wrote books in all the major classifications of the Dewey Decimal system, the only author ever, I believe, to accomplish that feat. I was well-versed in many disciplines and I was generous with my knowledge. I was blessed with a quick mind and an organized mind. Anything I learned I never unlearned. It was always there and always retrievable.

I remember one young woman who needed to know where the center of mass was in the earth/moon system. Now, many people believe it to be somewhere between the earth and moon. That is what she thought, but it turns out that it isn't between the two bodies. In fact it is inside the earth. A somewhat counterintuitive result, but that is the fascinating thing about the scientific endeavor, is it not? We learn things that are true, but that contradict our intuition. The young woman in question thanked me profusely for my knowledge. I was like a volume of an encyclopedia to her.

But the point is that you did not approach me with a question. You just wanted to tell me that you had read one of my books. I believe it was *The Gods Themselves*, and you were so excited by the story that you wanted to tell me so.

Such a curious book. It did not fit into any of my futures. In my last few years, when I attempted to unite all of my science fiction books into one grand scheme, *The Gods Themselves* stubbornly refused to be included in my plans. It was independent to such a degree that I had to admit defeat and put it aside as a completely self-contained work, with no tendrils of influence over my other works.

It also occurs to me that the book has some relevance to your current situation. The heroes of the book are trying to wake up their world from energy depletion by tapping an energy source in another dimension. Is not being in a coma like being in another dimension? And are we not trying to tap the energy of your mind to bring you back from that coma? Merely a thought that I present to you. Use it as you wish, or ignore it. I offer it with no expectations.

I remember how much you liked the book. As I listened to you, I remembered how it was when I was a young man, just discovering science fiction in the pulp magazines of the day. I would read a story I particularly liked and I wanted to tell the author how much the story meant to me. I wrote letters to the science fiction magazines praising writers I liked. So I understood your impulse and understood, as well, how much courage it took to make the effort at contact. You had no way of knowing that I would talk to you. Me, a famous writer, deign to give more than five seconds of my time to a mere fan? How could you know that such a thing was possible? You did not. And so, I listened to your faltering sentences and your gasps for breath with a great deal of sympathy. It was as though you were talking to God, was it not?

Of course, I accepted your praise with grace and as much humility as I could muster. That book received very good reviews and won several awards, which, of course, I found extremely gratifying. But in truth, reader adoration, for me, always trumped critical acceptance. The critics, you know, believe that they are writing for the ages. They pass judgement on books with an eye to posterity. They try to figure out what people will consider great in the future and adjust their opinions of books accordingly. But readers don't see things that way. They just want a good story and don't care if your books are going to be read a hundred years in the future. Such an attitude is good for a writer to be exposed to. There's nothing wrong with writing a good story that readers like. And if critics find the work wanting, well, that's their problem, not yours. And certainly not your reader's, either.

So I thanked you for your kind words. I could tell you were a young man, by your voice and your way of speaking, so I asked you about school. You told me about your chess playing and your grades. You were captain of your chess team. Your team placed second in a recent tournament. I congratulated you. You were good at math, which I told you I envied you for, since I had long ago reached my limit at math. You were a little surprised by this, but it was not false modesty for me to say so. I really wasn't very good at math. I learned what I needed to learn for my academic degrees and for my lectures in biochemistry, but calculus was it for me. Beyond that, math was a murky incomprehensibility. Some genius, huh? But you loved math and I told you that was wonderful, that you should pursue your talents and interests to wherever they took you. That is exactly what I did with my writing and my life and it took me quite far indeed. Not that I ever neglected the duty of family and making a living. For example, I remained a professor of biochemistry for a long time after I had established a lucrative writing career. Such cautious living was only prudent. One did not want to become destitute in one's life. That would not do you or anyone else any good. So I encouraged you to keep your grades up and go onto college and study a useful discipline that could provide you with a good living.

Do you remember any of this? I don't think you called me for my advice, but that is what you got from me. Was it useful? I hope so. If you found my voice beneficial to you then, perhaps you will find it beneficial to you now. I can hope for nothing more.

It was your wife who contacted me and said I might be able to help you out of your current predicament. Forgive me if that sounds mysterious. It was not a séance sort of thing. She did not raise me from the dead. She found some old paperbacks of mine stored away in your attic. You had saved them, so she thought I might mean something to you. She also found that old hardcover of *Gods*. Presumably that is what convinced her that I was some kind of childhood hero for you.

Am I? I think so. The evidence seems to indicate that I am. If it can help, then I hope so. I have heard of people in comas waking up for no explicable reason. It is a mystery. There are corroborated accounts of such things happening long after doctors have given up, so I suppose anything is possible. I understand, from the literature, that even people in comas can understand some of what is going on around them. Particularly voices. So you might be hearing my voice. I hope so. The world is full of surprises.

For example, I never thought there would be an afterlife. All my mortal days, I was convinced that human life simply ended upon death. I wrote about my belief with no hint of doubt or reticence. It seemed obvious to me that all the talk in religious circles of afterlives and souls and energy transference and ghosts and life after death was a lot of futile hope. Religions seemed to prey on this predilection that people had to believe in something after death. But, you see, there was no evidence.

I might just as well have believed that the Greek gods were real. There was as much evidence for them as for life after death. No, I was convinced. There was no soul. No afterlife. No transfer of vital energy. No reincarnation. Nothing.

So imagine my surprise when I died and this whole next phase of existence presented itself to me. I was shocked and pleasantly surprised. I was never so happy to be wrong about anything as I was about that. And it is a lesson you can use. Maybe you believe you are in a coma from which you cannot emerge. I can understand your reasoning. Indeed, before my death, I might have reasoned the same way. So many people in comas never return. Why should I be any different? But you could be different. You might be the exception. What does it hurt to believe in such things? Even death is not what I thought it was.

Not that I was happy to die. I wasn't. I would have gone on living forever if I could. Writing my books and stories. You know I spent eight hours a day at the typewriter. For years. Later I got a computer, but it was the same thing. I typed for hours at a time, putting down my stories and essays. Many people would consider that a wasted life, but not me. I had this insatiable need to tell stories.

I only hope some of this is getting through to you.

Perhaps you would be interested in knowing how she contacted me? Would you like a story?

I'll try. But, alas, one of the things that happened after I died is that my storytelling ability atrophied, somewhat. More than somewhat. A great deal, if truth be told. Storytelling appears to be a trait of the mortal realm. For what reason this might be so, I cannot say. I suppose that it might have something to do with survival. Mortals need stories to survive. They learn things by telling them and hearing them. Maybe. It is something of a puzzle to me, one I am still investigating. In any case, we do not appear to need stories in this realm. When I was alive, plots and characters would come to me with a frightening facility. I merely had to put my fingers over the keys and stories poured out of me. No longer. Nowadays I have to remind myself that I was the author of hundreds of books and at least as many short stories and who can even guess how many essays. Most of that is gone now, so please forgive me if I do not live up to what you remember of me. The thing is, no one lives up to that. No one can. In the afterlife, we are something less than we were.

There is a company, in California I believe, which undertakes to recreate the voices and personalities of deceased individuals. They use material in the public domain, and concoct computer simulations of us. They could do one of me, for instance. Not that they did. I mention it because your wife, Melody, noticed an ad this company had placed in a magazine she was reading and it gave her the idea to call me out of the void. She is a remarkable woman, but you, of course must already know that. She can call forth the visibles *and* the invisibles. Such a talent.

She was so determined in her quest that I could not refuse her. I am here at her bidding and at your service. This monologue of mine is for you to use in your efforts to rise from your comatose state and rejoin the world. You know, you have that option. Which I don't. I cannot come back. I cannot return to the corporeal world. I already mentioned that, didn't I? Ghosts? Forget about ghosts. There are no such things as hauntings.

Is this helping? They tell me you had a friend in high school, some-one who shared your interest in science and science fiction. Chris? I think you mentioned him when you called me to praise my novel. You said he liked the book too. In fact, you bought it together, pooling your money for the hardcover as soon as it came out, instead of waiting for the paperback. I found that quite touching, that you had a friend like that. It is good to have friends. I was lucky enough to have many friends when I was alive. Now I don't have quite so many. In fact, who am I kidding? I have no friends here. None. I'm alone. Completely alone. I miss my children, especially my daughter. I miss Janet. She understood me as no one else ever did.

Surely that means something to you? Your childhood hero, the man you looked up to, the one famous person in the world that you actually called on the phone and talked to, that person is telling you that the only important thing in life is the people who care about you and want you back. That should be enough. Crawl out of your coma. Do it for your wife and children.

I suppose I shouldn't overstay my welcome. In any case, I believe I have said what needed to be said. I was prolific in my time. I produced millions of words. I never regretted that life. But I also knew when to stop. I was famous for my concise and clear style. So many said I had no style, but a transparent style is not such an easy thing to cultivate, let me tell you. To write in such a manner that a reader instantly understands the meaning of a sentence, paragraph, or essay. Such a skill is not as prevalent as one might think. And not so easy to do. I spent hours a day perfecting it over decades of work.

But listen to me. I do go on.

This was supposed to help you out of your predicament. I hope it does. It would be nice to be able to do something for someone from where I am now.

Keep an open mind.

And come back.

Wake up, young man. You have the rest of your life waiting for you.

sally lane

Your wife Melody and I, we just had a long conversation. You married a very persistent woman. I feel as though she has the divine spark in her. I'm sure you feel it as well, so I will not dwell on it. I merely bring it up to let you know that I see it as well. It allows us to have some common ground. Without common ground, there can be no communication. At least in my experience. And I am being asked to communicate with you under the most difficult of circumstances. Consider: I have no way of knowing if you can understand me, or even if you can hear me. And you have no way of telling me if you want more of my words, or if you would just as soon that I left you to your inner world.

It is a dilemma. But Melody believes I can be of value. Therefore I have left my sanctuary, with my master's permission, of course, and am prepared to give you an afternoon, in hopes that it will aid you.

I should probably introduce myself. I am currently known as Sister Sally Lane. You will not know me by that name. Before I entered the order, I taught applied mathematics at the University of Waterloo. I was then known then as Professor Lane. You took one of my courses on your way to becoming an engineer. I have no way of knowing if you remember me, but Melody seems to think that I might mean something to you. Apparently you mentioned my class a few times to her over the years. How I brought the subject alive to you. That is very flattering. I confess that I cannot return the attention. In truth, I do not recall you. Not your name or your appearance. I hope you can forgive me for that. I had many students during my life as a professor. The ones I remember are the exceptional ones, the ones who excelled. And also, the ones who performed dismally. The two ends of the bell curve. The vast middle, well, most of those are forgotten, or, at best, a blurry muddle. I'm sure I am not telling you anything new. You must know that you weren't one of the stars, and also that you weren't one of the low achievers who shouldn't have been in the program in the first place.

So this conversation, this *monologue*, must be a generic thing. I'm to prompt you with memories. Perhaps even my voice, as Melody hopes, will revive some spark of life in you. I share her hope. Not in the same way as she does, since her life and emotions are so invested in you, but still, as one human being to another, I do hope you will come out of this and soon.

Wait. I think I may recall who you are. Yes. It's coming back to me. In one of my lectures I alluded to a quirk of quantum theory in which one could, if one had the requisite energy, figure a way to tunnel through time, as it were, and see the past. It was a tossed off remark, of no consequence to the substance of the lecture, but it sparked something in you. After the class you approached me as I was gathering up my papers and preparing to leave for my next class. I could see that you were shy. Bashful, even. You found it difficult to talk to me, I saw that right away.

Professors become quite good at figuring which students are bold and which ones are reticent. We use that, you know. We adopt ways to protect ourselves from the bold ones. They will monopolize your time, if you do not impose limits. But you were not one such. I could see that immediately and so I asked if you had any questions. And you then launched into a somewhat lengthy explication of your theory that even if we had time machines, there would be no way to ensure that what we actually saw in the past was the true past. You outlined your theory that if two people undertook to tunnel through time to a particular point in the past, they would each see completely different things. Their own decision to tunnel back would affect what they saw. You even offered a quick mathematical justification for your theory, based on quantum uncertainties and the constraints on the construction of the machine. In only a few minutes, you showed that time travel, like memory itself, would add fabrication on top of the truth, layers of it, so that we would never know which of those layers corresponded with actuality. Oh, my. When I think back on your words now, the purity of their vision still enthralls me. Perhaps you recall that conversation. It was so long ago, but it was a vivid thing. I think about that conversation, even now. I had simply forgotten that it was you.

Time machines. Such enchanting fantasies we entertain in our youth. Although, in truth, it was not so much the fantasy of such machines that intrigued me at the time. It was your enthusiasm for them. The way the very thought of them animated you to some emotional height that I could only observe.

But then, as I remember, you felt embarrassed. I did not know why. It may have been that I did not respond as you had hoped. Maybe you thought, since I brought up the subject in my lecture, that I was as intrigued by the thought of such machines as you were. It was not the case, of course, but I did try, at the time, to mirror at least some of your enthusiasm. It is a polite thing to do. A way of connecting, one human being to another. Still, I may have been wanting in that effort. If so, I apologize to you. Many years too late, but I offer my regrets as a gift.

After you talked to me, your ideas would not leave me. I thought about them for weeks and months afterward. If time and memory are so fluid, so subject to interpretation, it begs the question of who we are.

I pursued that question and could find no answer. This troubled me. I felt there should be an answer of some kind.

Before long I lost my enthusiasm for my work. I could no longer muster the energy needed to lecture on numerical analysis or optimization research. I went through the motions. I was part of a vast apparatus of education. My charge was to give knowledge in the form of mathematical truths that students would use to support their structures. A very important job. Without solid foundation, nothing built will ever last.

Your wife showed me your ring, the one you got upon graduation. Made from the metal of a collapsed bridge, collapsed because of the failure of an engineer's design. Such a curious tradition, to remind graduates of failure. But I saw the point of it. It was a call to never be the agent of such failure again. I came to think the tradition of that ring to be profound. You do not wear your ring. Melody told me it was because you do not like to wear jewelry. Most men don't. But you still cherished it. You still believed in what it meant, that doing a good job is more than important. It is a calling.

So I was one turn on the road to getting that ring. I had helped many students over the years. I felt good about my work, but then I began to have doubts.

I began to think that we were, perhaps, building too many things.

Perhaps it was time to stop building and simply appreciate what was already available to us, the natural world, made by the master builders of the ages: the sun, the trees, the wind, and the oceans. The earth itself, hot ball of iron with a thin crust. I think of what we live on: a volatile magma, barely cooled enough to form a crust for life. Perhaps you think of such things as you tinker with your drawings and bring concrete structure to fruition. Or perhaps you don't. It could be that such thoughts would cripple your creativity.

It did for me. The more I thought about training engineers, the more I considered what it cost me to continue to contribute to creating a class of people who were second-rate creators, at best, when compared to the master builders of the planet and the solar system, indeed, the entire galaxy and cosmos. The more I thought about it, the more I realized I needed to find something else to do with my life.

Ah, this is odd, to encounter the young man who set me on my current course in such a state as you find yourself now.

So let me continue. It is possible that if you knew the full extent of your influence upon another, you might prod yourself out of your predicament. Or it could be that you want to be in this state. I cannot tell, of course. If you prefer this state, if that is your calling, then I suppose there is nothing I can do or say, or *not* do or *not* say, that will change any of that. Nevertheless, I made a pledge to your wife. So I am here to tell you a story. A tale. Something of my life. Perhaps my life does not warrant such a grandiose term as story. My master always warns against pretense. Such is the life of an apprentice in our order. Pretense is much frowned upon. Although we do love the passive voice. You may have noticed. It is a way we have of removing ourselves from the world.

Yes, and we are criticized for it. We make no judgments regarding this criticism. If some have the calling to judgement, the need to appraise, evaluate, and examine, then it is not our place to stifle such a calling. All entities have their natural ways.

In any case, I am wandering. My master warned me that leaving the compound might result in such loss of focus. I begin to understand what he meant. I feel we are kindred spirits indeed. You have removed yourself from the world, as I have. We have done so along differing paths. But still. My master says there are no questions to be asked. If we ask questions, then we are not on the right path. I am full of questions. All the time. But I do not express them. Questions do not illuminate. They obscure. When I have released myself from all questioning, then I will have attained enlightenment. I wonder what such a state will be like. Perhaps it will be as you are now. Perhaps you are an enlightened being.

I find such a thought alien. It cannot be. And yet, it may be.

I wander, I wander.

I will return to a focus. Here and now. I am here. You are here.

You may recall what happened to me at the University. Some of it even made news in the outside world. A scandal involving a student. I was supposed to have slept with him. In exchange for a good grade.

Such nonsense. Nothing of the sort ever happened. Now, I am not so naïve, nor was I then, to think that such activity did not occur. Of course students and professors had relations. Such goings-on are as old as formal education. Surely Plato indulged his desires with his own students in the first academy. But I never did. I tell you this not to elicit your admiration or praise. Such is not my intention. Instead, I tell you this so you will hear the truth in my voice. I was framed by an administration that wanted me gone.

You may wonder why they wanted me gone. Ah, that is complicated. I made some overtures to the other female professors on campus. I wanted to organize us to fight against the injustice of the pay disparity between men and women on campus. Surely there could be no adverse repercussions to such an endeavor. Oh, but there were. I was singled out and made to understand that my efforts were not appreciated. I did not immediately see the extent of the machinations assembled to stymie me. I went blithely on my way, signing up fellow women professors to my cause. And then, like a bolt from the blue, I was accused of violating my terms of employment, and branded a troublemaker. Once such an accusation is in place, it is difficult to remove it from the public mind. I was tainted, and I knew it. Everyone on campus knew it. Overnight, I found myself without friends or allies. Men and women both, they shunned me and I found myself alone.

Couple that with my increasing disenchantment with the very profession of teaching and my inability to muster the requisite energy needed to fight the accusations, and my course became clear.

I resigned my position and left the University. I thought my life was at an end.

In fact, it was just beginning.

I moved out of my apartment in Waterloo and went to live in Toronto, a much bigger city, where I could be as anonymous as I wanted to be. And I did want it. I lived in a huge apartment building. So big that no one wanted to know anyone else. At first I found this state of affairs to my liking. After all, people had pushed me out of my life. People had turned my life upside down, in fact. So I didn't want any contact with people of any kind.

I sense that you may be in a similar position. You may have slipped from the world for the exact same reason. But let me continue my story. You will see that things turned out differently than anyone might have imagined.

I went on in this isolated state for a couple of months. I was feeling sorry for myself. I reviewed what had happened to me and could not understand why I had been treated as I was. It all seemed so incredibly unfair. I fantasized about slipping back in time and changing the events of my life on campus so that they led to a more positive outcome in my current life. That led me to remember your words about the malleability of the past, about how time machines, if they did exist, could not guarantee the truth of what they revealed.

Such thoughts, such words, your words, had a profound influence on me. I began to see that even though the past had been unkind to me, it didn't matter because it was only one past, and there was no way to understand if it was *the* true past.

I hope you see how you have helped me.

I began to read esoteric books on souls and knowledge. Truth and the search for enlightenment. I saw that my situation was not unique. Many before me had had the foundations of their lives destroyed and found themselves crumbling on uncertain ground. And where did they turn? To debauchery, some of them. I do not judge. To art and culture, others. Again, I do not judge. The making of things is important to people. I see that. I do not share the impulse any longer, but I see it.

If you could see me now, you might easily understand the path I chose. I am wearing robes. Rags, some might call them. I feel no shame in them. There is no reason. I find discarded clothing and cover myself with it. I find discarded food and eat it. I arrived here on roads that you, perhaps, had a hand in building, but I did not employ a car of my own. I have long ago divested myself of such things. I own nothing. Even the rags I wear are only borrowed from the earth. I walked here from the compound. I have not yet achieved enlightenment but I am well on the path, for I have gone perhaps one-one-hundredth of one percent of the way. It is a profound and beautiful distance.

Ah, but you see, I have given myself to boasting. Such lapses in humility, my master informs me, will happen here. He has such wisdom. I never question it.

I saw a message on the bumper of a car as I walked to this hospital. Such a benign institution. When you wake up, if you wake up, you should consider designing such buildings. It can be good for the soul, to bring such a place as this to reality. I hope you think it so. I hope you will consider it.

Now I have lost the thread of what I was saying. Such scattered thoughts. So many thoughts. Too many.

When I first began to investigate the path to enlightenment, it was a foreign place to me. So foreign that I did not know the turns and the signs. They looked to me to be riddles designed to stymie and confuse me. So I retreated again, into my apartment, where I watched television and ate uncontrollably. It was not until I became so overweight that I disgusted myself that I resolved, yet again, to seek something different from life. And so, in my enlarged state, somewhat cushioned from the cruelty of life, I embarked on a pilgrimage to a lecture at the local YMCA given by the man who would become my master.

The lecture was a revelation. Not in the sense of revealing the world to me, but in the sense of revealing myself to me. I realized that I was full of questions and that these questions, far from bringing me joy, only served to torment me. I decided right then and there to give up questions.

I have faltered some in the years since. But I do not berate myself for this. It is a normal part of my existence as a human being. Nevertheless, I strive for a semblance of being a human being free from inquiry. You will notice that striving is allowed. We strive. But we do not question. They are very different things.

Some months after that first lecture I approached the master and told him that I wished to be part of his community. Since I presented my request in an appropriate manner, he agreed to allow me to do so.

I now live in a community of about a hundred people. We are men, women, and children. Some have called us a cult. Such terms do not trouble us. We are removed from the general buzzing of the world, but we are part of the world, as you can see. I have come to this place to assist you.

I have also, I now realize, the need to thank you. To thank you for your initial talk with me, so many years ago. The talk that led me to my current path. Seeing you, comatose and without reaction, makes me think of some of my other students, the ones who never reacted in any way to my lectures. It is amusing. That life was so long ago. The formulas and concepts, they recede from my memory. It is as though they have all gone to sleep. I can feel them there, still, under my brain. It is a strange feeling, to know that though they are insignificant to me now, they once held what I thought to be the secret of the universe. Little marks on paper. Equal signs. Integrals. Numbers and letters. Symbols of my older profession.

Well. Enough of that. I believe I have come to the end of what I can offer you. If you can hear me, if you can understand, I want to let you know that life is not such a great mystery. It is not about the paradox of time travel and memory. It is not about building things. There are too many paradoxes already. There are more than enough built things in the world. Life is about acceptance.

Can you understand that?

lisa mcdonald

Oh my, you look so sad. I'm sorry to blurt that out, but seeing you like this. It's startling.

I brought some children's books to read to you. Melody said it might be something that you could use. I know your parents have passed, so we couldn't ask them what stories they read to you when you were a kid. Melody says you never much talk about your childhood. That's okay. Most men don't. My husband never does. It's like men are born when they're twenty-one. Their women have to dig into their past. You are archeological projects for us. Ever think of that? And now you are the ultimate project.

Melody and I cried over you before I came in here. She says she got my name from Chris Pratt. That's a name from my past, I can tell you. I asked her if she let Chris in here and she said yes and I wanted to tell her how awful that was. Chris was an awful young man when we were in high school. I never understood how you could be friends with him, because you always seemed like such a nice boy. Kind of kept to yourself, which was fine, but still, a nice boy. Chris was never anything like that. We dated a couple of times. Silly, calling what we did in high school *dates*. We had no idea. He got grabby with me a couple of times, even after I told him to stop. So then we didn't go out anymore.

I feel like I should be talking about high school days because that's the only thing we have in common, really, but I wonder if it means anything to you. I don't think about my time in high school much. Does anyone? I suppose some people do.

I wanted to go out with you. You probably don't remember that at all. I waited for you to ask me, but I figured out soon enough that you were never going to. And I never did ask you. I suppose girls do that sort of thing now, but not then. Not that I ever saw, anyway.

But really. Don't you remember the notes I left on your locker? Probably not. Probably you just thought they were a joke or a prank or something.

Well. After high school I went to college. Studied art history. Oh, yes, I had my eye on the job market, obviously. My parents didn't understand why I would do something like that, but I thought if you didn't indulge your flights of fancy then, when would you ever? Most people end up married with children. It's true. They do. Not so much anymore, maybe. People are more independent now, but it was definitely true in our day. When we were young people. Since I loved art, I wanted to immerse myself in it while I could. And that's what I did. And then I met Mark, and we got married, and we had children. See? It was pre-ordained. I'm so glad now that I got my degree in what I really wanted. My life with Mark is a good one. Our children are all grown up. You had your kids late, I see. I'm going to be a grandmother soon. I can't wait. You'll have to wait for that, it looks like. Oh, I hope your kids want to have kids when the time comes. There's nothing better than being a grandparent. I love it already, and I'm not even one yet! How crazy is that? I work at the art museum now. I'm in charge of putting on exhibits. I love it! Do you ever go? You should. I know you're an engineer and all that, but it would do you good. Even engineers have to understand beauty and art. Maybe engineers more than others, since what you make is so out there. Not out there, weird. Out there, as in everyone sees them. People can't avoid seeing what people like you do. They live with what you design.

[clears throat]

Oh dear. Do I sound like I'm lecturing? I don't mean to. I teach some classes at the community college sometimes and I do tend to lapse into a lecturing voice. Just ignore me.

[pauses]

Well, maybe it's time for a story. I found some from when my kids were toddlers. Ones I remember they liked. Actually, this will be good practice for me, since I'll be reading stories to my grandchild soon.

Here's an easy one to start with. *Goodnight Moon*.

[reads *Goodnight Moon*]

Isn't that something? Such a simple story. Not even a story, really. Not sure what exactly it is, but the art is amazing. You can't see it, but trust me. Oh, why am I even telling you this? I'm sure you read this one to your kids, didn't you?

[pauses]

I'm sorry for crying. I told myself it wouldn't do you any good. But I can't help myself. Give me a minute, I need to find some Kleenex.

[pauses]

There's some.

[blows nose]

Melody set up this digital recorder. She says she wants to keep all these talks that people are giving to you. A kind of sonic album. Maybe she'll play them over to you. Set them up in a continuous loop.

Melody is so devoted to your recovery. I'm sure you probably already know that, since you've been married to her for twenty years, but it is astonishing to watch. She showed me all the people she has lined up to talk to you. Incredible. If this talking cure has any possibility of bringing you back, the way she's working it, it will succeed.

My kids always liked hearing stories again and again.

So here we go. *Goodnight Moon* again.

[reads *Goodnight Moon*]

Did you hear it that time? I sure did. I haven't read this in ages, but when I got to that page without the illustration, where it says: *Goodnight nobody*. Oh, that just makes the book, I think. To acknowledge the emptiness, but to make you feel like there is more than emptiness. Or that the emptiness is not frightening. It's benign. It's a place to put yourself, your dreams and your desires.

Oh, listen to me, going on. It's just a children's book. Surely the author didn't think about all those things when she wrote it, did she? Or maybe she did.

It makes me think of where you are. Is it a big nothing? Or is it something? The biggest something there is? This is so hard. I don't know if I can keep going. It's like a conversation, but not really. I know you're not ignoring me, but it feels like you are.

Isn't that crazy?

I've been around people who make you talk to them. Have you ever? It's strange. You don't want to say anything. You have no intention of talking, but then you are around them and all of a sudden you want to tell your complete life story. Or tell them your deepest secrets. Your fears. I know how they do it. They use silence. It'll happen at parties sometimes. Or receptions. Art receptions, especially. I go to a lot of them to keep up on what's current. It's important to my work. You don't want to end up out of the mainstream of contemporary art in my business because you can be a has-been in no time at all. Art is skewed to youth, you know, and we don't have a lot of it left, not at our age.

Was that a joke? Sometimes I make jokes and don't even realize it. Never mind.

I was saying that certain people make you spill your guts to them. They make silence into something bad and you feel like you need to fill the silence so you do, and when you do you use whatever you have at hand, which is usually yourself. Anyway, what I'm getting at in a convoluted way is that you, lying there like this, with the silence, not like the silent page in *Goodnight Moon*, which is a good silence, but *your* silence, a bad silence because it means you are not completely there, that silence, it needs filling, so I'm filling it.

I never saw you at any of the games. The football games. I went. I tried out for cheerleader, but I didn't make it. It was just as well. I really didn't want to spend all that time practicing. But I still went to the games. I had school spirit. It was so important. Remember how we used to have pep rallies for the players? That was so much fun. We took five minutes off every period through the day so we'd have this chunk of time at the end of the school day where the whole school would get together in the gym.

Oh my gosh, that was so amazing. Everyone yelling and screaming for the team. Where were you? I looked for you but never found you.

I remember once I asked where you had been and you said something about how you were on the chess team and the school never had a pep rally for you so why should you go to a pep rally for football.

Oh, I suppose you're right. There's too much attention paid to football, and I sure didn't want my son to be in football, and I'm glad he wasn't. They get knocked around, you know, and it affects them. Their brains. It's awful that schools even have football, but back then we didn't think about that. You didn't either, if we want to talk about the truth. You didn't care about the safety of the players. You just wanted to make a point about your own activity.

Fair enough, but I think you missed out on a lot. You know, if you had gone to the games, we could have spent some time together. I know that's all water under the bridge, but I wonder, did you ever notice me, even for one second? A half a second? Something?

There, you see? I have to fill up the silence.

I actually thought of putting on a pep rally for the chess team. But, really, think about it. Who would come? You were all a bunch of nerds! I don't mean to offend, but it's true. You were. Can you even imagine anyone from your team walking out on the stage and listening to the school cheer them on? It wouldn't happen. You wouldn't have done it. Or if you had, you would have walked out with one of your sci-fi books in your hands and you would have read it while you stood there. You would have! You know you would.

So no pep rally for you.

I wonder if I felt sorry for you. Spending your time in the quiet so much. Quietly reading. Quietly playing your games. Maybe you like where you are now. Maybe being so quiet is what you want?

No, no. The way Melody talks about you, you are not who you were in high school. Well, who is? Maybe Chris Pratt. I'm sure he's still grabby with women. Never married, Melody told me. Lives in Las Vegas. Doesn't that say it all?

Oh dear. I don't want to judge him. It's not my place. It's just that his life seems so empty.

But not yours. You became something. You have a good solid job. I suppose the nerds are the ones who keep the world going. They like all the infrastructure. Then people like me come on your roads and we fill up your buildings with beauty. Have you ever thought of it that way? You're the worker bee, and people like me, we're the queen bees. We labor to make the life in the hive. The hive being your buildings and your roads and all the other things you engineers put together for us. The bridges. The cities, really. All built by you.

[pauses]

You know, in some ways, it's like I never even went to high school. The memories are so distant, so foreign now. High school is a place my children went to. Coming here and seeing you, being reminded that I, too, went to one, well, it makes me think I used to have a secret life.

[pauses]

Let's try *Goodnight Moon* again. I can see why children like to hear stories over and over again. It's very soothing. I hope you find it so.

[reads *Goodnight Moon*]

Now that time, I was able to concentrate on the pictures more. They're very primitive. I can't tell if they're primitive in a sophisticated way or in a naïve way. That's very curious. I should know that. After all, it's my field.

I remember when I used to read this to my kids, they became so still. They would not move a muscle. It was almost as if they *could not* move a muscle. It was the most amazing thing I had ever seen. Of course, it didn't last. After all, it's a short book. But for those few moments, it cast a spell. An amazing spell.

Maybe I'm making a mistake by reading this book to you. Maybe you are still enough and you need something that will knock some will to move into you? Isn't that why I'm here?

I have all these other books. A pile of them. I had planned to read them all to you, but it's getting late. I'm getting tired. I sandwiched you in between some work meetings. I'm working late this week, putting the finishing touches on a new exhibit.

You would probably like it. Right up your alley. An exhibit of M. C. Escher. Do you know him? I'm sure you do. Those crazy perspectives, all those strange faceless people walking in circles or living in impossible buildings. It turns out there's a collector right here in Toronto who has dozens of his prints in excellent condition. He inherited them from his father and is perfectly willing to lend them to the museum for a few months so we could mount this exhibit. I think we will draw people from all over the world. They're an enigma, these pictures. They cast a spell. Just like *Goodnight Moon*, I suppose. Maybe that's what lasts in art. The things that we can't understand completely. They make us want to go back to them. Like children hearing the same story over and over. We play over our memories like we have nothing else. Like all we are is our memories.

So.

Anyway.

I do want to keep talking, but I'm getting tired. Not from the talking, from the thinking. You aren't making it easy for me. You, sir, are not keeping up with your end of the conversation.

I really think you'd like the Escher exhibit. Tailor-made for nerds. We actually talked about that when we discussed putting on the exhibit. We brought up the perennial problem of getting people into the museum who normally don't go to museums. And we thought of technically-minded people. They like Escher. It's the one artist they can identify with. I even suggested an exhibit of blueprints at one time. Blueprints can be very beautiful. The detail in some of the ones I've seen is remarkable. I can spend hours with them, going over the lines and letting them float into my brain, creating the buildings in a virtual manner.

I suppose you have to have that skill, don't you? The ability to see the end product from a drawing? I admire that. I do. It shows not only a strong imagination, but a social meaning beyond yourself.

I want to read *Goodnight Moon* again. I do! Isn't that crazy? For all I know you're in there screaming at me. Please don't read that book again! Please please please.

Okay, I won't.

[pauses]

I don't know what else to say to you. Melody will play this over. I want to offer you something. I want to make you want to be alive. Do you want that? Of course you do. Your children are still young. Your wife loves you.

She does. I can see it. And why wouldn't she? *I* love you, for goodness sake. Or loved you. I don't think she would mind me telling you that. Not love, I suppose. A crush. A school girl crush on a boy who was so far away, so unattainable, so oblivious to me.

I have no regrets, you know. I would not go back and change anything. It was good for me, the way you had no interest in me. It taught me a very important lesson, that life does not always give you what you want. That wasn't a lesson I wanted to learn when I was a high school girl. Not even a lesson I think I was conscious of then.

I went to one of your tournaments. Did you know that? Probably not. I wasn't there for long. They're boring to watch, especially if you don't know the rules. You have to agree with me on that. But I was there long enough to see that you were completely in your element. It was amazing to see you in your chair, sitting across from your opponent.

You commanded the room. You filled it up. All the other players could see it in you.

I never understood sports. Still don't. Games where people throw balls around or knock things into holes or hit them with sticks and bats. So futile. Even though I loved the pep rallies and the school spirit, football, the actual *game*, just seemed silly. Still does. Where is the beauty? But at that moment, so many years ago, seeing you with the pieces arrayed in front of you, and your brain working, clicking, eyes maneuvering, the *essence* of you completely *there*.

That may be when I first had an inkling of what true beauty is: the ability to *be* completely and utterly in the moment.

You gave me that gift, even though you had no idea.

That's why I came here today.

To repay you on some level. In some small way.

To offer my gratitude.

scheherazade

I am told that my fame has outlived me. How can this be? You are not of my time and country. This place is foreign to me. What are these bare white walls and these contrivances surrounding you? I see boxes, shiny. And lights. The sighing of machinery, if machinery it is. Or is it magic in those boxes? Are there genii living in them?

I may not even be real. Am I the manifestation of some wizard's imagination? Calling me up for his amusement? Indeed, are you such a one? Are you more cunning than you appear, inert and dumb on the bed before me? My king was such a man. So filled up with hate and revenge in his heart that he could not be moved. Not for many months, though I told him tales.

And why does my history still live in this age? I come from a time and place when killing a woman, merely for being a woman, was not a crime. Indeed, it was common practice for a king who tired of his wife to dispatch her to the empty realm and no consequences befall him for such an action. Not just kings. Men of lower class, even the lowliest of the low, could indulge such murderous impulses with impunity.

But history changes things, does it not? My tale, one of desperation, one in which I concocted tales as a way to outwit a wicked king, has become a charming legend, when in truth, as I lived it, it was a terrifying and soul-slaying time.

You know that the king forced himself upon me? Your legends of me do not make that clear. He made three sons by me in this way. Finally, after I had exhausted my tales, after I had birthed for him three children, then and only then, did he consent to let me live.

Let me live.

In all my stories that I told to him, none was so fantastic, so incredible as my own tale, the tale of how I became a queen.

Your versions of my legend make it clear that I volunteered to be his consort. Oh, how the blind eye of history mocks my life. Why would I volunteer to put myself into such jeopardy? I did no such thing. I was snatched up from the streets by the king like a common dog and made to appear before him for his night of debauchery. Can you conceive of any sane person, any sane woman, putting herself into such a situation? If you can, you have a more expansive, a more profound imagination than I ever employed in my survival.

No, it was only my quick-witted thinking, on the spot, that allowed me to propose to the king that I might tell a story before my death.

You know the rest, of course. I stopped my story before the end, feigning weariness. I told him I could not go on. The king granted me a day's reprieve that I might finish the story the next night. Such a kind-hearted soul, no? Bah! He wanted to hear his stupid story, one I made up about a king and a genie and, oh for goodness sake, who knows? It was a ridiculous tale, born of desperation. My professed weariness did not prevent him from raping me that night. Nor the subsequent nights. But that bit of my tale is missing from your legends, is it not? Too awful, I suppose. The reality of what happened to me might spoil the charm of my tales, is that it?

On the next night I finished the first story and immediately launched into a second. I stopped before the end and the king indulged his desires upon my body again. And so our life together proceeded in this way, night after torturous night. I desperately wracked my brain for a new story every night. Sometimes I remembered old tales my mother had told me. Sometimes I made up new stories from my own imagination. Other times I told about my family. My kind sister, my timid brother. Everything I ever knew, all the people I had ever met, they all went into the ragbag jumble of my storytelling. It kept me alive, yes, but what a life. I thought of death. Longed for it. But life has different plans for us sometimes. Life can be stronger than our own impulse for a preferred existence.

The king was an awful man who held my fate in his hands. One night I told him that if he raped me again, I would not finish the story the next night. Do you know what he did? Do you think he relented and left me in peace? Do you think he acquiesced to my humanity and allowed me the dignity of leaving my body unmolested? He did not. Instead he beat me. I was carrying his child at that time, the spawn of his evilness, and he knew it, and still he beat me for the crime of attempting to assert my own worth. I was bloodied and bruised by him.

Over the course of our nearly three years of my telling stories and him listening, I was assaulted nightly. I birthed three of his children. I confess I did love them, the children, but I despised him, the king, all those days. He did not wash. His breath was like the wind from a camel's corpse. Vermin lived in his beard and cavorted in his hair. I caught diseases from him.

But I lived. Yes. By telling stories.

Your legends say that he fell in love with me. That I taught him the value of love through my stories. That I taught him how to be human. Such was not the case. He kept me alive for the children. That is all. After my stories were done, I do believe he had grown used to me. His sons adored me: who does not, as a child, adore their mother? That was enough for him to marry me, thus making me his queen, and giving me some rooms in the palace that I might pass my days in some comfort and be allowed the privilege of raising my children.

He continued, after my days of storytelling were done, to take concubines to his bed. A new one each night, snatched, as I had been, from the streets, or from the houses of ordinary citizens. Truly, from wherever his whim suggested. If I can claim any kind of victory against him, I suppose the only plausible one would be that after me, he deigned to allow these women to live, whereas before his time with me, he had killed his nightly conquests after his rape.

You see that I did not save only one life, mine. I saved many more lives after me. But do not then conclude that the king was a fine man. Do not make the mistake of thinking him a wise and fair man. No. I believe he simply grew old and weary. It is a state we all succumb to eventually. Indeed, as my sons grew, as I kept them from their father as much as possible, and as the king grew older, he sometimes approached me with a certain gentleness. It was as though he harbored some sense of apology towards me. I never, however, asked him for such. I did not feel it my place to make him see the wickedness of his life. If, indeed, he wanted, in his old age, to understand what he had done, that would have been all to the good. But how could anyone, given his history, given all the women he had violated and killed, how could anyone, contemplating the enormity of his crimes, truly accept their culpability? I suppose such an acceptance might lead to one's death. So he never did. And I never steered him in that way. I shunned his overtures to me. It was my only defiance, the sole power I had at that time.

I sought escape from the palace. Several times. With my children. And even, once or twice, to my eternal shame, without them. I was willing to leave them to his court, unprotected by me, simply so I could escape bondage under him. Do you think me wicked for such actions? Perhaps so. Our instinct for self preservation sometimes makes us less than we should be.

But escape proved impossible. None in his court dared defy him. Therefore, I never had any allies. And who could blame them? The king was known to order executions at the slightest pretense, as one might flick a spider off one's shoulder. I never escaped. My sons grew. Eventually they became young men.

They were devoted to me. I taught them the fruits of our culture. I educated them in languages, in history, in art, and mathematics. They learned the art of cloth making, the craft of cooking, and the habit of proper grooming. I taught them to sing, play music, and tell stories. Yes, my one true talent, I passed on to them. They became fine young men, a thing not to be underestimated in my time.

But the influence of the king could not be denied. One morning, when they were no longer children, but not yet men, he snatched them from their rooms and put them into service in his army. He had decided he needed a war for his amusement. And so he threatened a neighboring king. Can you conceive of it? The ridiculous man had used up his diversions and needed the excitement of conflict.

Or perhaps he concocted the war for the sake of his sons. He knew my love for them had taken them from him. His only way to bring them back to him was to turn them into warriors.

When I woke and found them gone, I believe I knew, in that instant, what had happened. I ran to the king. I found him in his chamber, still in bed with a young woman. I flew at him and pummeled his chest and slapped his face.

His eyes blazed. He was unused to being shamed in such a way in front of one of his victims. She rose and wrapped herself in a blanket and ran off. What a story she would have to tell about a crazy woman coming to interrupt her pillow talk with the king.

The king stood up to me, stood on his two feet, confidently, as one who commands all he sees around him. He took my beatings until I had no strength left and slumped to the ground, tasting sand, and I put my arms around his ankles and begged him to let his sons return to me. I did not want them to become soldiers. I did not want them to die. He had the whole kingdom to recruit soldiers for his war. Why did he need my sons?

Can you envision the scene? Sadness overwhelms me even now as I recount it to you. I feel the grief in my heart. I feel the coldness in his heart, a freezing night cold that no warmth could penetrate.

He kicked me aside, then calmly informed me that young men needed to be toughened up. He had given me many years to indulge myself and my values upon them. He thanked me for my work, for my efforts at civilizing them. But the final portion of their education, the part that would turn them into true men, would have to be his. He needed to teach them the warrior arts. Surely I must understand.

I wept. I cried openly and sloppily. I told him they were all I had.

You can imagine my hopes at that point. I desired that I might melt his heart. I wish that it were so. I wanted him to be like a genie bottle, that I might touch him and magic would pour forth from him, and I might have my wish. I dared to allow myself the possibility of such a resolution to our awful story. Please. Show one tiny scrap of pity. Is it too much to ask?

Indeed, it was too much. He refused me completely. He clapped his hands and two guards came and dragged me away and threw me into my room and bolted the door.

Do any of your legends about me tell this part of the story? Do they recount how I undertook a hunger strike over the next few weeks, refusing any kind of nourishment until my sons were returned to me? How the news of my defiance reached the king's ears and how he then undertook to force food upon me? Three strong men held me down and forced open my mouth and poured raw eggs into me. I fought. I scratched and kicked.

I wished, with all my heart, that one of my children had been a girl. He would have left her alone. He would have at least let *her* be with me.

But fate, that indifferent potency, did not give me that comfort.

Eventually I gave up my protests. Through all the years, I had been defiant. Through the pain and savagery, I kept myself whole, somehow, but as time went by I grew too weary of fighting. Such outcomes curse us all, I'm afraid. My storytelling gave me no comfort. My education held no joy for me.

My sons went to war, as decreed by their father, the king. I did not see them off. The king would not allow it. I was held captive, as he decreed. I heard the soldiers, on the other side of my wall, marching by. Their swords shivered the air. My own body felt the electricity as they went by. It was an awful feeling, for I knew what it meant. My beautiful sons had become fodder for *his* war.

Shall I stop the story here?

That is how I extended my life, day after day, for years. Is this not why you conjured me from the depths of legend? Do you not want to hear stories so that you might wake up, so that you might live?

This story has an ending. Most stories do. Your story will end as well. Probably not today. Or tomorrow. But someday.

I feel as though I owe you something. Why do I have this feeling in my heart? Because you gave me this late life, this small cork of existence on some mysterious sea of time?

Are you a wicked man, like my king was? I know nothing about you. I can only guess. There are many in this structure who work to keep you alive. That should count a great deal in your favor. But the king had many such in his palace. They indulged his every whim. They fed him and cared for him. They made sure he was amused. This did not mean that he was a good man.

So you see, I do not know if I should assist you. I do not know if you are worthy of an extended life. Perhaps I should remove all these accoutrements of the healing arts of your time and allow you to live or die on your own. How can one be said to be alive when one is part of a machine?

It is the unknowing that is most difficult. Perhaps you find it so. Did I upset you with my tale? The tale of my life? Did I spoil some rosy-hued picture you had? It was not my intention to cause you distress. I merely wanted to tell you the truth. Storytellers, though they make up their tales, are always interested in the truth. Do you not find it so?

Very well. The truth. Or, at least, a version of it.

I feigned sickness. In my chamber I pretended that I had a terrible pain in my stomach. A healer was sent in to see to me. An old and dim man. If he ever harbored true skills as a healer, those days were long gone. He examined me carefully, prodding me gently, as gently as he could, while I cried out in pain. He said that I had internal damage, that there was nothing he could do for me. I begged him to allow me to see the king, one last time, that I might say goodbye to him before I died. He was eager to please me, so he said he would bring me to the king. As we walked to the king's chamber, I pretended to be losing my strength and hung onto his shoulder. As I did so I worked my hand around his back and removed the dagger from his side and slid it under my robes. At the king's chamber, the healer escorted me to the bed. I laid down on the blankets and asked the king to come to me. The healer told the king I was gravely ill and that he should be kind to me. Then the healer left and the king, completely flummoxed, hardly knew what to say or do. My love, I told him, come to me. Lie beside me. I miss you. I need you in my final hours.

What could have gone through his head then? What did I say that turned his heart? How did pity enter him? I do not know. But he came to me. As he walked, I moved my hand to the handle of the dagger, and when he was close enough, I sprang from the bed, dagger held high, and I plunged it into his chest. Blood poured from him. His face froze in astonishment. He fell to the sand. I fell upon him. I pulled the dagger out and plunged it again into his chest, then into his belly and finally drew it across his throat. By this time blood was everywhere. It warmed my hand and stained the sand. All his strength seeped out of him with his blood. He never cried out.

I was the queen. All the king's subjects must now answer to me. I immediately ordered his generals to retreat. I made peace overtures to the neighboring tribes. I sent them chests filled with gold and jewels. The war ended.

My sons returned to me. We lived in peace and harmony all the rest of our days.

Does this story give you what you need? Did I end it too soon? Should I have waited?

Perhaps I will return tomorrow and tell you another. Will you stay alive for that? In your sleep state, will you still be here, waiting?

You should.

Because everything I told you is a lie. I never feigned illness. I never stole a dagger. And I never killed the king. In my imagination I did so thousands of times. Millions. But not in my actual life.

No. The war raged on for years. Men on camels slicing each other up with their swords.

My sons returned to me, one by one, dead. I buried them. The king allowed that courtesy, to be at the gravesides of my sons as they were put into the ground.

The king defeated the neighboring tribes. He took their land and their wealth. He killed all their leaders and enslaved the population. It was just the victory he needed to make his life complete.

And then, when my sons were gone and his war was won, my king, my foul and most vile king, my eternally contemptible husband, he came to me. While I stood before him, he bent down on one knee and bowed his head.

And he thanked me for making my sacrifice that allowed him to make his life full.

And I, filled with hatred, could do nothing but wait for him to lift his head. Such a curious look on his face. An apologetic gaze, as though he knew he had wronged me. But I saw beyond the look. He did not care that he had wronged me. Would never care what he had done to my body and to the fruits of my womb.

I drew my chest high, I pulled phlegm from my throat, and rolled it over my tongue and spat it in his face.

robert hawken

Mom, he can't hear me.

[pauses]

Because I know. His brain isn't working. You said it yourself.

[pauses]

Okay, I *get* it.

[pauses]

I'm waiting for you to go, Mom. Please.

[pauses]

This is so weird. Dad? Man. Mom wants me to talk to you. She's got all these people lined up to talk to you. It's crazy. She's like, on this major project to bring you back. She asks me, don't I want you back? Well, duh. Yeah, I want you back.

I guess.

I don't know. What if you want to be there, where you are now? You know the accident was all in the papers and stuff. You're like famous.

Oh, yeah, and I got into a fight over you. At school.

Do you want to hear any of this?

Mom says just to talk. She says you might be hearing it. I don't know if it's true. Some guys at school said you were like this vegetable and you'd never come back. They said guys like you, in comas and stuff, they just—after a while—they just kind of die. Is that what you want?

Shit.

Oops. Sorry. You don't like me cursing. Neither does Mom. Well, guess what? Kids swear. You guys must have sworn too. I know all the swear words. You want to hear them?

Because, come on, we hear stuff. We use stuff.

This is so fucking weird.

Oops again.

[laughs]

Mom wanted me to tape this. I said no. I said I'd talk to you, but not if they were going to tape it. Also, not if she was going to be here. It's hard enough, man. Talking to a vegetable. Shit shit shit. You're never going to wake up. They're right. The kids at school. I could say anything I want. Everyone you ever knew in your life could come in here and talk to you and it wouldn't make a bit of difference. I could use every swear word I know, every swear word ever *invented*, just to get you riled up, but it wouldn't matter. Would it? *Would it?*

No. It wouldn't.

I got a bloody lip. None of my teeth got broken or anything. I hate dentists.

How it happened was there's this guy at school. He likes to pick on me. Not just me. Everyone. Bullies. Man, they are the worst. The absolute pits. I wouldn't mind just getting a magic wand and making all the freakin' bullies of the world disappear. See, I can stay away from the swear words when I want to. Freakin'. That's not so bad.

But anyway. Like I told you, you are, like, all over the news. Everyone in school knows about your accident. How you got hit by that truck. Do you even remember it? Maybe not. Maybe it hit you and you went into your coma and nothing about it ever registered. I don't know. *I don't fucking know.*

Shit. This is just way way way fucked up.

So. I'm already the lowest of the low in high school, you know. Grade nine. I'm like the maggot of the school. All ninth graders are. They call us maggots. Sometimes fewmets. Which is shit, if you didn't know. They think that one's real clever. I can't wait to finish grade nine. It sucks so much.

But anyway, this one bully. I don't even know his stupid name. I *purposely* don't know his name because he's such an asshole. Every day for, like, weeks, he stands by the cafeteria door and waits for me to come by, and he asks me about you. Only in this sucky way. He asks me how my vegetable is doing. That's you. You're the vegetable. Get it? Then the next day he says something like is your dad going to be in a tossed salad soon? That way he might be of some use to society. *Real* witty. Yeah. I kill myself laughing over his wit. Then the next day it was pasta primavera. He asks me if you are going to be in a pasta primavera. Then the next day he says how's your compost pile coming along? That's you again. He's saying you're so far gone that you're compost.

So each day I pretend that I don't hear him. What else do you do with bullies and jerks? But after a while, it gets so old, and he's *such* an asshole I can't just ignore him anymore. I can't.

Mom tells me I shouldn't pay any attention. I get it, I get it. I do. Really. But Mom isn't there. None of her friends tell her she's married to a vegetable, you know. None of the people at her work make these crude comments about you to her face. They don't. So she doesn't get it. I know she's my mother and everything, but she doesn't get it. She doesn't know what it's like.

She said she would go talk to the principal about the asshole bully.

Oh, God. Why do parents always think they can fix things by talking to the teachers? That *never* fixes anything. It only makes things way *worse*. About ten times worse. Because then you will always be the wimp at school, the guy who couldn't fight his own battles. The guy who had to have his mommy come and fix things for him.

If that happened, I would just have to go to another school. I'd *have* to. You'd have to let me. I told all that to Mom and I think she kind of got it, but she was still mad. She still wanted to fix things.

But she did listen. At least a little. Enough to let me deal with it.

I was going pretty good. It had been close to two weeks. Every day the same thing. I didn't let it get to me.

But one day I walked by him. I was ready for whatever he had to say.

Then he said only an asshole would desert his family the way you did.

Dad, I don't know why that got to me. But it did. I gave him the finger. That's all. I swear. Nothing else. Just the finger as I went by him.

All he had to do was ignore it. He didn't have to do anything.

But he did do something.

He grabbed my hand and bent back my finger. Guess I got him mad. Didn't take much. He's, like, insulting me every day, and I do one thing back and he can't take it. He bends my finger way back. Not enough to break it, because I kind of bend my arm back so he can't get the right angle on it, but my finger hurt.

Then it was like everything changed. Something about how he was trying to hurt me. I got this, I don't know, this crazy feeling in me. I couldn't control myself anymore. My head felt hot. It was like something else took over me. I had some books in my hand and I threw them down on the floor. Threw them so hard the cover bent. He pushed on my hand harder. I bent over further and then I was on the floor. But not for long. I got this rush of adrenalin. It filled me and I jumped up and hit. I hit him hard. I punched him right in stomach. Then I punched him again.

Kids all around me stepped way back. I've seen fights in school before. It's always the same. No one ever tries to stop them. None of the kids, anyway. They always let the guys fighting get on with it. This was the same way. They made a circle around us. Right there in the cafeteria. Crazy. But I knew it wouldn't last long. A teacher would come out soon and pull us apart, you know. Outside, in the yard, the fight could go on for a while because the teachers are never outside. They like to hide in their staff room. But in the school. You got only a few seconds to get in your hits.

So I did. I tried to hit this guy as much as I could.

But, Dad, you know, I'm not a fighter. I'd have to learn a lot to become one, because I'm just not. I don't know how to do it.

I wanted to. I wanted to real bad, but my hits didn't bother him a bit. It was like a flea hit him. My fists just bounced right off of him.

Then he grabs my hair and lifts my head up. Oh man. Right then and there I thought I was going to die.

This is so weird telling you all this.

[pauses]

Mom said it would feel good to get it out of my system. She said you would have a hard time hearing all this if you were awake and everything, but I should take advantage of your situation so I could tell the whole story without you giving your two cents about it. Okay, she didn't actually say, like, *two cents*, but you get what I'm saying.

[pauses]

This guy punched me right in the eye, and then he punched me again in the lip. I started bleeding.

I'm not sure exactly what happened next. I got dizzy. I think that's when the teachers came over and grabbed him so he wouldn't hit me again. I heard him say I started it. Yeah. Like I would start a fight with him. Like, I do that kind of thing everyday. Oh yeah, that makes sense. A whole lot of sense.

So they pull him off. And blood is pouring down my chin and onto my shirt. I'm still mad, you know. I can hardly see because my eyes are all blurry. I'm still ready to jump on him. If I had something to hit him with, I would have done it.

Dad. If I had a gun right then, I would have used it. I would.

See why I don't want to tape this? See why I don't want anyone hearing it?

Except you. If you can even hear.

[pauses]

It is up to you. You're the dad. You're supposed to be the smart one, you know. You're kind of like the guy who's supposed to keep me safe, you know. I've been thinking about that a lot since the accident. Mom cries every night. Do you know that? No. You don't know anything right now. But she does. Laura and me, we don't know what to do. No one does. She has her friends and she says she has us, but what she wants is for you to wake up.

[pauses]

I don't even know what I'm talking to you for.

[pauses]

So anyway. The bully, he's kicked out of school. For I don't know how long. A week. Only I'm kicked out of school too. For fighting. That's a laugh. I didn't fight. I punched him with, like, the weakest wimpiest punches in the history of punches. You know? He never even felt them. Plus, *I'm* the one who got his lip bloody. Not him.

But they have this rule at school. If you're in a fight, any kind of fight, even if it's not your fault, then you have to get suspended.

That is so unfair. It is. You can't tell me it isn't. Like, in real life, if some guys get into a fight, then they don't both go to jail. They figure out who started it and everything, and then that guy might go to jail, but the other guy, he's like doing self-defense. He's just protecting himself. That's all I was doing. I was just keeping him from breaking my finger. Or trying to.

So anyway. I'm out of school, but I still have to do my homework and everything. I got a friend bringing it to me. I don't want to do any of it. It all sucks. Plus, what if I don't do it? They going to kick me out of school? I'm already out, you know?

[pauses]

I went to the hospital. I got four stitches on my lip. It's still all swollen and everything. I'm going to have a scar. The doctor says there's not much he could do about it. He asked me what the other guy looked like. Big joke. Sometimes grown ups are such . . .

Well, they're just jerks.

He thought he was being so funny. I was like, to myself, shut up you jerk and just fix my lip, okay?

Mom was there, standing beside me. I thought she was going to start crying, but she didn't. That was cool. It was bad enough that she was there with me while I was getting all sewed up and everything, but if she started crying, man, that would have been embarrassing. I would have wanted to just die. Right there. Go into a coma. Like you. Ha ha. I can make stupid jokes, too, you know. It's not just the stupid bully and the doctor. Anyone can make stupid jokes. It's, like, the easiest thing in the world, okay? So easy a vegetable could do it.

[pauses]

So, Mom was right. This was easy. I thought it would be hard. It's like talking to the computer and it can't talk back. Cool. I told you the whole story and you couldn't come back and make me feel like I told it wrong.

[pauses]

I don't know if Mom wants Laura to come talk to you or what. She's like super nervous about it. She told Mom she wasn't sure if she could. All her friends are like helping her out all the time. They come over and they all do things. Like sit around reading magazines and stuff. Or they eat ice cream. Mom says it's good for her to have friends at a time like this. They help. She says I should get together with my friends.

But, you know what? None of my friends feel like coming over and talking about nothing. It's like I'm too weird now because I have a father who is dead but not dead. They're weird about it, I know they are. But it is weird. It's way weird what happened.

If you ever wake up, I wonder if you'll remember any of this. Probably not. One of the doctors told Mom sometimes when coma people wake up, they don't have much of their memory anymore. Or they have it, but it's all different. Distorted. He told her that so she could be ready for it. But, personally, I don't think it would be any big deal if you woke up with different memories. Everyone has different memories, you know? I remember stuff from when I was a kid that Laura remembers different. Like, she says I picked on her sometimes. I said I never did.

So who's right? We asked Mom and she said we had to work that out between us. We had to come to an agreement.

Well, it's just crazy. You can't agree about what happened if you think what happened is different than what the other person thinks happened.

It's crazy. It's weird.

[pauses]

Oh, man. It's weird. Mom is at the door. She's looking through the window. Checking up on me, I guess.

[pauses]

[laughs]

I just waved to her and she turned all red. It was like she thought I didn't know she was there. That's funny.

I'm going back to school day after tomorrow. I don't even know if I want to. I know, I know. I have to. Yeah, I *get* that, okay. It's not like I'm going to not go to school. It's just that I'm saying I could do without it. It was weird being at home while everyone else was in school.

Maybe Mom's right. Maybe I should have more friends.

[pauses]

Okay. She's at the door again. She probably thinks I'm recording this, but I told you, I'm not. I held up the little recorder she got. It's got, like, room for about a hundred hours. She's going to try to fill it, too. She says when you wake up you can listen to all the things people told you while you were asleep. I guess you might want to do that. I guess. I don't know. I don't think I would want to. Who cares what people told you when you were asleep, after you wake up? It'd be like listening to dreams or something and that's pretty boring. Dreams are. At least I think so. Mom says dreams are important, but she was talking about other dreams. About things you wish for in your life.

But you must want to wake up, right? You must want to get out of your coma. So that's a dream. I guess. I don't know.

[pauses]

So, okay. When you wake up I'll look different. I'll have a scar. You told me once I shouldn't get into fights. Fights don't solve anything.

I don't know. That might be one of those things adults say that they want you to believe but that isn't true. Because I think my fight did something. It made that jerk bully leave me alone. I hope. I don't know yet, but I hope so.

Sure. It's gotta mean that, right? He's not going to come after me anymore now that he knows I fight back. Right? Isn't that how it's supposed to work? Even if I had wimpy punches, he knows I'm not going to take his shit anymore. Doesn't he?

x hawken

Waaa waaa waaa.

Hey, you remember that? That sound? The crying sound.

Where are you?

[pauses]

I'm still blind. I can't see you, but I feel you there. You got out. Good for you. Of course, you killed me to do it. Not your fault. I get it. Just one of those things.

[pauses]

Still. Any of these people who've been telling tales around the campfire-that-is-you, any of them know you're a killer? Probably not. Mostly because, I guess, *you* don't even know it.

[pauses]

Ah, shoot. Didn't want to go all victim on you. But here it is, for what it's worth: the truth of me and you is that you're a twin. I'm a twin. I'm *your* twin. Only thing is, you killed me before I was born. Yeah, you killed me in our mother's womb. It wasn't anything personal. I guess. Who knows? So, the thing of it is, I went directly from the time before birth to the time after death. No in-between time for me.

None.

So you gotta take that into account when I tell you that I don't have a lot of sympathy for you, you know. You at least had a few decades in the living realm. In the grand scheme of things, it's only a tiny sliver, you know. How do people put it? A drop in the bucket? Yeah, that's it. Your life is a drop in the bucket. My life isn't even a drop.

You ever miss me?

There's lots like me where I am now. We float around. Bump into each other. We have this language we invented. I'm using it now, so I don't know if you can understand any of it. But, hey, twins have their own secret language, don't they? That's what people always say about us. Or about the ones who survive.

I heard about these birds. When the eggs hatch, the baby birds, they get into these fights. Over resources. Food. And they throw each other out of the nest until only one of them is left. The biggest one. The strongest. Nature can be a bitch, sometimes. The survival of the fittest shouldn't mean that you kill your own siblings. But it does. Like with the birds, the biggest one gets all the food because he's killed all the others. So now he gets to grow up and have babies. Darwin explained it all, didn't he? Did you know some of his kids died when they were real young? Probably not. People like me, the ones who never got born, the ones who got *killed* before we got born, we're pretty attuned to such footnotes in history. Makes you wonder what he thought. Did he think: *Okay, that daughter of mine died. Guess she wasn't fit, so it's just as well. That's natural selection at work.*

Hard to imagine.

No, he must have been devastated. His science training probably didn't turn him into some machine, working through his theory by way of his children. Probably. But who knows? Who can say what goes on in someone else's brain?

Like yours, for instance. What's going on there? You want to die, is that it? But you don't have the guts to go through with it, so you take this halfway measure.

Tell you what. Change places with me.

Here. Let me nudge you out. Here I come. This can work. We're twins. We have the same mental map, you know. I could take over your body. I'd wake up. Darn right, I would. I want a taste of some of what you took from me.

[pauses]

[some labored breaths]

[longer pause]

Oh.

Hey.

Well, you're a lot stronger than I thought. Don't want to turn over the controls, huh?

[pauses]

Well, okay. The story of my life. Always in second place. Fine. I get it.

But let me ask you, why'd you toss me out? Mom was too small, is that it? She didn't have enough nutrients for both of us? I'm not buying that. Lots of twins get born. Sure, lots of them don't. Lots end up like me. Believe me, I know. We have this club, like I told you. Or maybe I didn't.

Oh, I lose track of things. You don't know what it's like. You spent all that time acclimating yourself to life. Me, I've been acclimating myself to death. To nonexistence.

Here's the thing. I could teach you a lot. You're kind of nonexistent now. Do you even realize that? You're in a different country. We have different rules here.

But I need one thing from you first.

I want an apology.

[pauses]

I know you were young. You didn't know what you were doing. I get all that. If I was in your position, I'm not sure I would see the need for an apology either, but I don't care. I want it.

[pauses]

I'm not hearing anything.

[long pause]

[sighs]

I think maybe I'm not getting through to you. There could be a language issue. But I'm you. You're me. We shouldn't *have* to learn each other's language. We should have the exact *same* language. We should be able to communicate with no problem whatsoever.

I'm going to go ask some of my friends.

Wait here.

As if you can do anything else.

[pause of several days time]

I'm back.

Waaa waaa waaa.

Baby talk, huh. You remember it?

Waaa waaa waaa.

It has a certain poetry to it, I think. Primal. Like the first Om. I hear the Om all around me. Do you? Maybe not before, but now you must.

What else is there? Me yammering away in your ear? That can't be any fun. Or profound. It's not like I'm connected to the divine.

Here's what my friends told me. They said I shouldn't even be talking to you. Do you talk to your murderer? they said. Do you talk to the person who took your life? Do you talk to someone who had no qualms about ending your life before it even started? They said that talking to you was like giving the enemy a pass. It was allowing the wrongdoer to get away with it and to even feel good about getting away with it because his victim actually wanted to be friends with him, and how sick was that? Pathological. I would be a victim all over again, every time I had any contact with you.

Now, even taking into account that they were all more or less predisposed to hating your guts (sorry, but it's true), I listened to their advice very very carefully. I weighed their arguments. They suggested I kill you, just like you killed me. I considered it. Some even volunteered to do it for me, if I was unwilling. I thanked them warmly. They are such good friends, but the job would not be so easy. For them or for me. Still, I suppose if we pooled our wills and our strengths, we could do it.

But here's the thing about victims.

We don't want to kill.

Revenge is overrated. We know what it is to die and we don't want to be a part of it.

My friends, they talk a big game, but if it came down to it, I'm sure they wouldn't stoop to revenge either.

So what I did is I thanked them for their advice and told them I would think it over and if I needed any help I would definitely recruit each and every one of them in my campaign. My campaign to dispatch you.

Then I went off and got depressed for a while. Because you didn't help me. Do you realize that? You popped into my life, what was left of my life, and you gave me some kind of weird hope. Like we could be siblings again, *real* siblings, you know. The kind that *talk* to each other and do things together. Things *besides* not letting the other sibling get born.

[pauses]

I'm losing it. I know. There's still a lot of bitterness there.

Mom never knew. How could she? I was there, in one of the early ultrasounds. Just a blur. Hardly even a ghostly gray smudge in the murky blackness. That was before you strangled me. You were already a lot bigger than me. Maybe it was inevitable.

I confess, I wanted you gone too. From the womb, I mean. I felt you there, so big. You were *hungry*. You wanted it all, everything that came down the tubes. How'd you get so much bigger than me? Maybe you just started splitting cells just a fraction of a second before me. Was that it? That tiny head start, completely insignificant at the beginning, accumulating into something big as the days passed? Maybe cell-splitting has an extreme sensitivity to initial conditions? Probably that was it. It wasn't your fault. It wasn't anyone's fault.

But it still feels like murder.

Because when you got big enough, you arranged things to your liking and you didn't care about me. I got shunted aside. I ended up shriveling away. You remember *any* of this?

No. Of course not. No one remembers the hurly-burly of life in the womb. You get born and that's all gone. In the deep deep past.

But me. That's all I have. I never experienced any of life's hurly-burly, you know. It was all there, inside our mother. That's the sum total of my existence.

[pauses]

You should be dead. Really. In any other century, you would be. The only thing keeping you going is all the attention you're getting. Oh, I suppose there were probably coma patients in the past who woke up after a long time. But not too many, I bet. Not too many that made it through months or years. They mostly just slipped away. A lot of them probably got buried before they were even really dead. People just figured: this guy hasn't moved in days. Must be dead. Let's bury him.

Is that how it was for me? Did you say: this guy hasn't challenged me in days, he must be expendable, let's just kill him?

[pauses]

It's like nature is the real murderer here. Don't you think? It's not you, not really. You didn't know what you were doing. I get that, I do. There's a certain instinct that we all get born with. Your instinct was to survive. So was mine. It's just that mine wasn't as strong as yours.

[pauses]

Do you like having a name? That's one thing I miss. We don't name each other here. Not in this realm. A lot of people wear their nonexistent names like a badge of honor. It's as if they *want* everyone to know that they have no significance in the world. Defiance. It's a potent emotion.

[pauses]

Some of us, we go back to things over and over again. We remember life in the womb. Some of us remember touching our twin. I remember it. It's why I can't hate you. Not really. I had my hand on your cheek. Lots of times. I reached out for you. And we were starting to get fingerprints and fingernails. Just beginning to assert our identities. We were identical twins. Did you know that? Yup. But not exactly identical. We didn't have the same fingerprints. Maybe that's what turned you against me? That little difference? Before that I was a mirror image of you, but after that, you saw a flawed mirror when you looked at me?

I don't know why I'm still trying to figure it out. I should let it go.

[pauses]

I don't want to be pathetic. Who wants that?

[pauses]

Well, now that I think of it. Maybe you. Yeah. Big baby that you are, lying there on the bed. Waaa waaa waaa. Look at me. I'm all half dead. Don't you pity me? Don't you feel sorry for me?

[pauses]

Why am I even here, floating around you? What have I got that you want? Can you answer me that? Can you say *anything* at all? *One thing.* Just say one word. One syllable. A sound. Waaa.

[pauses]

Waaa.

[pauses]

Try it like this: Waaaaaaaaaaaaaaaaaaaaaaaaaaaaaa.

Draw it way out. It'll make you feel good. I promise. I did it a lot back then, when I first died. I wanted to get born. I wanted to take the breath of the world. You need to do that. You need to wake up. Take in the world for both of us.

It's a start. That's all. Just make the start.

I bet it would work if you weren't here. They're doing too much for you. If you were back home, you'd want to be alive. Really, who would want to live here, in this fluorescently lit, sterile environment? It's repellent. How do they expect people to get better here? I'm asking. Just asking.

[pauses]

Do you remember an imaginary friend from when you were a kid? Maybe not. You're not so good with the memories, I noticed. Kind of empty in that department. Anyway, that imaginary friend was me. I had to be about eight feet tall. Maybe more. I used to bend my head down to get through doors. Oh, yeah. You gave me a name. Charlie. You remember *any* of this? No? Then how come *I* remember it? Charlie was your invention. He was your only friend when you were a little kid. Come on. *Remember!*

[pauses]

You really are pathetic.

See, Charlie wasn't something you made up. Charlie was me. Well, not exactly me. My name's not Charlie and I'm not red and I'm not a rabbit. I'm not anything. But Charlie was what you wanted to be. Charlie was big and strong. And fluffy and cuddly. Plus, he stood out. He was your mirror image. Or the image you had of yourself.

You needed Charlie because you missed me. You had Charlie, but what you really wanted was me. Your twin.

[pauses]

Sorry to be the one to spill the truth to you, but it's true. You killed me. Yup. But you also missed me. You wanted me back. They call it this feeling people have that something is missing in their lives. There was something missing. Your twin. Me.

I'm pretty sure that all kids who have imaginary friends, probably had twins in the womb. They have to fill that emptiness. Which you did. Quite nicely, actually. It was a little bit deflating, let me tell you, to be replaced by a big fat nothing. Something made up in your head. But I saw it. Saw the wisdom of it, you know. Saw how it all made sense in the grand scheme of things. I actually, after a while, liked seeing you with Charlie. You were buddies. I wanted to be your buddy. How sick is that? You killed me and I wanted to be your friend.

I think I felt more sad about Charlie going away than you did. Remember Mom asking you about Charlie one morning? She wanted to know where he was. You told her he went on a trip and he wasn't coming back. Mom smiled. Are you sure? she asked you. Are you sure Charlie isn't coming back? And you told her he was never ever coming back. Never. And she asked if Charlie was okay. And you said he was okay. But then you asked her if Charlie was maybe mad at you. And our mother, our sweet mother, who nurtured me for weeks, for months, before you killed me, she told you that no one could ever be mad at you. Not for one second. That Charlie just needed to go away because he had rabbit friends he wanted to go back to and he would always think of you as his friend too and he wished you the best and he hoped that you wished him the best and maybe, maybe, Charlie would come back some day in the future to visit you.

You were a little confused about that. You thought maybe Charlie was a little strange to think of you as his friend, but then decide to run off without you.

But let me tell you, I was bawling the whole time she was telling you this, because it was like she *knew*. Even though she didn't *know* she *knew* about me. She knew that I was there. I could see it in her face, how she looked past you, to someone else, someone shadowing you. It was eerie and it was the best moment of my life. Or my non-life. Whatever you want to call it. Because in telling you about Charlie, she was telling you about me.

Get it?

Any of this sinking in? There's a whole big world all around you, you know. You don't see it, but it's there. Mom saw it. She knew.

[pauses]

A lot of people know. You could know, if you let yourself. But you won't do that. Even when you wake up—*if* you wake up—you won't remember anything about what I'm saying to you. We might just as well

still be in the womb. Us competing for resources, you deciding coopera-
tion wasn't going to cut it. All that will just fly out of your brain.

It's sad, you know.

Makes *me* sad anyway.

Makes me want to cry.

Waaaa waaaa waaa.

Baby talk. That's all I've got. All you've got, in the end.

Because where I am now, you'll get here someday too. I'm not
making a threat or anything. Don't think of it that way. Don't think of
anything in that way.

I talk big, but I'm not big.

I'm nothing really.

Just your twin.

Try to remember that.

If nothing else, remember that once you were two.

stephen jensen

[whispers]

Hey. I won't be here long, man. Just have to empty the trash and pick up a little. They try to keep the place tidy, you know? That's my job.

[pauses]

Don't know why I'm talking to you, except you're famous. You don't know that, but you are. Reporters were here today. From the newspapers. From the TV. Your wife is famous, too. Maybe more famous than you, to tell you the truth. She's got all these people coming to talk to you. It's like a crusade. So everyone wants to know about her.

And about you.

Now I know some things I didn't know before. Your dad was a miner. Worked underground up north. Sounds like a hard life. Your mom used to work in a store. A checker. Unskilled labor, just like me. We make the world go around and around, you know. People like your mother and me. If we didn't do all the stuff people didn't like to do, people would just die.

Anyway, that's what I tell myself. To make myself sound like more than I am. To me.

You're famous in the hospital, too. Oh, yeah. Real famous. Everybody wants to know about the coma guy. There's a pool going. Bet you didn't know that. How many days you're going to be asleep like this. People pick their number. It's been, what, thirty-eight days now, I think. I'm in the pool. I have day one hundred. Good even number. So if you wake up after 100 days, I win some money. How about that?

Your wife, man, she's got some kind of energy. She wants you *back*. What is it? You good between the sheets, or something? Is that it? You aren't so good right now.

[laughs]

It's the middle of the night here. Things are pretty quiet. Your wife went home to get some rest. You know, sometimes she's here for days in a row. Just sitting here talking to you. Or reading to you. When she can't get someone in here to tell you a story, then she reads to you. The newspaper if that's all she has. Because they're full of stories. She says hi to me. Nice lady. Sad. Her eyes are all puffy from crying all the time. She says hi to everyone. She asks everyone if they'll talk to you. Some do. Some of the nurses, they will talk for five minutes if they can. But they're busy, you know. They got patients.

None of the doctors will talk to you. Not one of them. They got this chip on their shoulder or something, I guess. It's beneath them. They're like on top of the heap. They got all this class privilege. They aren't going to do the hard work, you know? That's for people like me. We'll do it.

Me, I'm on the bottom of the heap, so I see it all. I see how the doctors push the nurses around, and the nurses push the orderlies around, and the food-service people, they got almost no status, and then there's me. Bottom of the heap. That's okay. Someone has to be there. May as well be me.

Whenever I see your wife, I always make sure I'm super nice to her. She deserves it, the way she's devoted to you. Yesterday she asked me about my job, how I liked working in the hospital. That was nice. No one ever asks me how I am. I'm usually the invisible man, floating around with my wipes and spray bottle. But your wife, she's different. She cares about people.

So I told her. Not much. I didn't tell her my troubles or anything, not about how my wife is. She's sick. Fighting the cancer. Doctors say she should be okay, but it's rough. Anyway, I told her a little bit about my wife. Not a whole lot, since she's got a lot on her mind, but she didn't let me get away with that. She wanted to hear more. So I told her. And she listened real close, like it was important to her. Maybe it was. I don't know. Maybe she needed to take her mind off you. After, I told her it was nice to talk to her. She said it was good to hear my story.

That made me think. She said story. She didn't say it was nice to hear about my wife, my family. She said *story*. I was going to tell her good night and continue my rounds, but I stopped and I asked her what she meant by that.

Well, I got an earful. Turns out she's been studying story. I didn't even know there was such a thing as studying story. I always thought story was just a story. It was just something you told kids. Put them to sleep. But she had this quote from some poet. She wrote it down for me. Let me get it out of my pocket and I'll read it to you.

[pauses]

Yeah, here it is.

The universe is made of stories, not atoms. Muriel Rukeyser. You ever heard that quote? Must have, since your own wife thinks it's the most important thing in the world.

But I asked her what that meant. I don't have a lot of schooling. I got through high school okay, but not much after that, and I don't do a lot of reading. But I remember in science class, they told us the universe was atoms. So what does that quote mean?

Your wife, she explained it to me. Or she tried. I didn't get what she was saying. It was all about that our perception of the universe is a story. It's like atoms are an illusion. But stories, that's what we live with. That's what we perceive, so that's what things are really made of.

I listened, but, come on. Those are just some words some poet put down, and poets, they don't know any more than I do. And everyone knows poets don't make any sense. If they did, then you wouldn't have to learn them in school. You could just read their poems and understand them, without studying them.

That's how I figure it, anyway. No one has to explain *Law and Order* to me when it's on TV. I watch it and I understand it. No one has to go to school to get *Law and Order*. So it's maybe better than poetry, you know? It makes itself clear.

I even said that to your wife. I said, well, *Law and Order*, it's got stories, don't it? She said yes. So I said, then the world is made of *Law and Order* episodes?

She laughed at that. I was glad I made her laugh. She don't do much laughing anymore. If she ever did. I don't know if she did, but it seems like she probably would. She seems like she's full of life.

So I left it at that. Neither of us thought the universe was made of television shows.

But it makes you wonder.

Stories. What are they?

I see lots of books in people's rooms. When I'm cleaning up. Mostly I see mysteries. Lots of people like reading about crimes. Murders. I don't get that. It always seemed weird to me. Here you are in a hospital, where people die every day. Where you could die, to put it honestly. And still, people want to read about people dying.

Maybe it's easier if it's someone else dying? You can read that kind of story and think, well, they're stupid for dying but I wouldn't ever die like that.

I don't know.

Crazy stuff to think about.

Guy down the hall, he told me he died on the operating table. He told me like I never heard that before. So I listened. He said he couldn't talk to the doctors or the nurses, they would make fun of him. I told him no, they wouldn't. They're trained to be nicer than that, even if they *want* to make fun of you, they don't do it. But he said I was wrong, so I said, okay, I'll listen to your story.

He was having problems with his heart. They had to put in a new valve. So he goes into the operating room, and they put him under, and about half an hour into the operation, he says he floated out of his body. He looked down and saw himself on the operating table, his chest all open and bloody. But he didn't care. He was free. It was like he could fly. He told me all this with hardly even taking a breath, like this was the weirdest thing ever. To him, it probably was, but not to me. Not to anyone who works in a hospital. We've heard the story a million times. He looked down on the surgeons.

Well, I tell you. I've been in that operating room. I know exactly what it looks like. I also put a message on top of one of the cabinets in the corner. On a regular piece of paper. I used red magic marker so it would be easy to see. In big capital letters I wrote: WISH YOU WERE

HERE. I did that a long time ago. Months ago. I check every couple of weeks, just to make sure it's still there. No one goes up there except me. See, I'm the cleaning guy. I'm supposed to clean up there.

I want to know if the stories people tell me about floating up, I want to know if they're true. If you really can float up, and look back down, then you should be able to see that message, right?

So I asked this guy, real casual, if he saw anything while he was floating around. He doesn't know what I mean. I told you, he says, I saw the surgeons. The tops of their heads. One of them was bald. The anesthesiologist had black hair. She wore white shoes. I saw it from the top. My feet were cold. They put slippers on them. I saw the slippers.

See, all of this, he already knew from before he was under. That's why I don't necessarily believe these stories. But I listened. I tried to push him to tell me what else he saw. He was getting a little irritated with my questions. Like he thought I was doubting him.

I *was* doubting him.

But finally, I asked him straight out. Did you see anything on top of the cabinets?

He got all confused. Cabinets? he said. What are you talking about, cabinets?

I said, from his perspective, which was way up at the ceiling, he should be able to look down and see what was on the top of the cabinet. He should have had a bird's-eye view, you know. If he was *really* there.

But he didn't know.

He couldn't tell me what the message said.

I went back, just to make sure it was still there. It was. That means it was there when he floated. Or thought he floated. So I was disappointed. I wanted him to have floated. It would be cool if things like that happened. But I don't think they do.

So I listened a little more, just to make him think I was still interested. I wasn't, but it would have been mean to him if I just walked away. He said after floating around for a while, it felt like hours, he started feeling a tug. In his belly button. He looked down and saw a white rope going from his stomach back to his body on the table. Back to his chest. And this rope, it yanked at him. Made him come down. Like the rope was a string and he was a balloon. He tried to fight it, he told me, scared-like. But the string was too strong. It reeled him in, just like a fishing rod bringing in a trout. And bang! He was back in his body.

I told him that was a great story and it wasn't weird or anything. Things like that happened.

Then he surprised me. He said he knew things like that happened, he wasn't stupid, what bothered him was that he didn't want to go back. He wanted to stay up there in the floating world, up there in the ceiling.

I said, what's the big deal?

He said, he wondered, did it mean he didn't want to live? Did he want to be dead? He was afraid to tell the docs because he thought they might think he was trying to kill himself.

Man. Things like that, I think maybe it would be better to keep to myself. Stay invisible. I said no way. It doesn't mean that, and then I tried to get away from him. What did I know about suicide? I'm just a janitor, you know? I don't know anything.

But he wouldn't let me go. He grabbed my arm. He really wanted me to tell him he wasn't suicidal. Hell. I was on the spot. I told him maybe he *did* need to talk to someone, if he had these feelings. He needed to get some help to just sort it through. I told him anesthesia does weird things to people. You need to wait a few days for it to wear off. Then you would be your old self again.

I told him all that.

I had no idea if he wanted to kill himself. How would I know that? But he thought I had some kind of smarts, just because I'm in a hospital, I guess. Just because I'm around smart people. Or people who think they're smart. I don't know. Being a doctor, you know, you have to have brains, sure. But I've seen some doctors who are jerks. Just because you went to medical school, it doesn't mean you're the greatest person who ever lived. They got robots now that can do some of that stuff that doctors do. I've seen them. They go into people. Sure a doctor guides them, and all, but still, the robot does a lot of the fine work. In ten years, it'll probably be some technician, some guy like me, who can push a few buttons and stuff. I'll be able to work that machine.

Ah, listen to me. Trying to make myself bigger than I am. That's my story, I guess. Always trying to move myself up the hierarchy.

But this guy, this heart patient. He really got to me. His story, it was hard. It was hard to listen to it. He was in some big distress. I told him to take more of his morphine. Put himself to sleep. Then it would all be over.

He said he was afraid to. He said he thought if he fell asleep he would float out of his body again and he wouldn't want to come back and he wasn't ready for that. He wasn't ready to die.

I pulled my arm away. I had to. He was making me nervous. Scared. I had to peel his fingers off my arm. One by one. It was awful, doing that, because the guy was in real distress. I could feel it. I could tell. He was starting to sweat. He was so scared. But he was making me scared, too. I had to get out of there.

You wanted something from me, he said.

I said, what?

He said, when I was asking my questions, they weren't just to be polite. They were to get information.

I said, yeah, so?

So, I should be willing to give back to him.

But, I said, but but but. I don't have anything to give back.

Then he got all quiet, like a pouty kid. Might not be nice to say, but that's what he was like. He sulked, like someone had taken away his toys. I've seen that look on my kids. I knew what it was. And then. And then. Suddenly, I saw it. I saw what he wanted. He just wanted to know that it was okay. That's all. He didn't need me to fix his life, or explain his experience. Who could, right? He knew that. Sure he did.

So I told him about my wife. About how sometimes, after the treatments, which are a bitch, let me tell you, she tells me that she isn't sure she can go on. And I tell her, I say to my wife, all sick and in pain, so different, but still there, you know, still under all the bullshit, the lady I married, she's still there, and I know she wants to live. I know she has life in her. And I tell her it's okay. I put my arms around my wife and I tell her whatever she's feeling, it's okay.

Sounds simple, right?

Maybe it is simple. Maybe not. Maybe it's the hardest thing in the world. I don't know. All I know is that after I tell my wife that, she can sleep. She doesn't get cured, but she can get some rest.

So I tell this guy, this heart valve guy, the same thing. I tell him, lots of people come out of surgery and they feel like they can't go on. It's not a big deal. If you have those feelings, it's okay. Just go with them.

I saw his eyes light up. A little. He uncrossed his arms. Let them fall to his side.

Then I ran out of his room. Sounds crazy, but that's what I did. Forgot my stupid supplies, so I had to go back in. When I did, the guy was asleep.

So I don't want you to think I wanted the guy to die. That isn't what this was about. I had this story to tell, you know, and I knew you would listen to the whole thing. Not judge, or anything.

I've got other rooms to clean up. Hope you get better. Hope you wake up. Hope my story didn't bore you too much. One thing it taught me, I don't talk much to patients anymore. I say hi, and that's about all. I think maybe I'll take down my message too. Who cares if they float up for real or if it's just a story they made up in their heads? Stories are real. If you think it's real, then it's real. Isn't it?

Is that what that poet was trying to say? That the only real things are stories?

Huh.

[pauses]

Or maybe she's saying all we are is our memories. And stories are just memories, things we make up. Both of them. Neither of them is real.

Makes your head hurt thinking about stuff like this.

Doesn't matter. I'll leave you in peace for a while. You could probably use a break.

Wake up on the right day, okay? I could use some extra cash.

a centaur

Ha.

Call yourself a human?

I'm more of a man than you, and I'm only half a man. Less, when you consider the mass of my body. A horse has a lot of muscle. A big belly too. It's all I can do to keep up with it, since I have only a human mouth. Eating constantly. It's my curse.

But you, lying there like a dead fish. What good are you? What possible use can you be?

Your sleeping brain conjures strange visions. Like me. Brought out of myth to your realm. Don't you have anything better to do?

Damnation. I have to take a piss.

[pauses]

Yeah, there's a lot of it. It's not my fault, so I won't apologize.

Someone will clean it up. There are maintenance people, aren't there? Well, as I said, I don't care. I'm here because you wanted me here.

What is the purpose?

[pauses]

I see. You cannot answer. It was as I suspected.

The smell of my piss do anything for you? I'm told my various odors, at various times, can wake the dead. But I see I am not waking you. Maybe because you aren't dead?

Here is the thing you need to know about me: I am the pure product of storytelling. I am not human, nor am I equine. You may think of me as tale. Born of tales. Or of tale-telling. In any case, pure imagination.

I feel my legs twitching. These muscles, they need room to *move*. And you have me here in this room. I don't even know if I can fit through that door.

Ah, it's like eternal damnation to be beholden to someone's dream, especially the dream of a comatose man.

Wake up, you bugger! Release me from this!

[pauses]

Wanker.

May the piss of a thousand centaurs shower you daily. May the shit of those same centaurs adorn your dining table and nourish your belly. May the sweat of a thousand more drown you. May the hooves of a million more crush you into the dirt.

May the...

Oh, what's the use? You can't hear a thing I'm saying. I may as well be talking to myself.

[pauses]

Is that your game? You're hoping to emulate me? What is your purpose, man? State it! For both our sakes, tell me why I am here.

[pauses]

Oh. How I long for the skies. Life was simple then. I lived in the cold and the darkness. Perhaps you have the same experience now? Maybe we are closer cousins than I thought.

In those long-ago days, I was simply some points of light in the sky. Constellations, you call them. Your imaginations. Oh my. What power there. They are your engines of life. It is how your kind meddles with the universe. You don't stop to think that the universe may not want to be meddled with. So strange. I existed in the firmament. Not a bad life. Eternal. Kind of boring, sometimes, to be in one place, but the spheres of life rotated beneath me. I saw the panorama unfold. It was enough. I didn't need to cavort in the meadows, as it were. But you, you imagining humans, you had different ideas.

Do you know, I didn't even realize what I was back then? I never connected the dots of the stars that made me up. If I did, I would not have seen any semblance of the creature you now see before you. I would not have discerned the human head, arms, and torso. No. Or the attached legs, tail, and body of a horse. Who would conceive of such a creature? An herbivore's bottom locked together with a carnivore's top? Ludicrous! Nature makes no such errors. One look at me and it is clear that I came of some demented power.

And so here I am. Plucked from the sky and brought to life. Or some semblance of it.

You have this strange power. You make me want to tell you a story. I never tell stories. I *am* a story. Have you considered what this does to an entity?

My brain should be connected to a whole human body. But it is not. *Your* brain commands a network of interlocking systems. You're born with a brain perfectly congruent with your network.

Not me.

My early days were awkward. Horses and humans have different growth rates. It was not pretty. When my horse section was fully grown, my body section was still only three years old. Hardly more than a baby, and I was required to operate this huge bulk of muscle and bone. Feeding me was a full time operation. I had to eat constantly. Fully two dozen wet nurses were employed to keep me alive. Can you conceive of it? Can your imagination, the thing that brought me here, does it have the power to understand even a little of what it meant to manifest me in this world?

I thought not.

Don't try to do it. Not in your condition.

I am told that I am belligerent. Crude. Nasty. Unpleasant to be around.

I do not deny it, but my disposition came of understandable origins. I was not only a stranger in your realm, I was a stranger to myself. To my two realms.

I became what one might call a juvenile delinquent.

It was a calling.

I reveled in it. I galloped wherever I cared to. I pissed and shat wherever I pleased. Whether it was in some old woman's flower garden, or in houses of worship, or in your swimming pools. I didn't care. People had to clean up after me. I trampled the ground where I went. Sometimes I would spend the entire night in one person's yard, simply trotting over the grass in circles, over and over, in a kind of meditative rage, until the yard was nothing but shitty pissy mud, roiled up into slick and disgusting peaks.

And then off I'd gallop to somewhere else. I kicked at things. My hind legs were powerful and I loved that power. I stood with my tail to a window, and I'd kick the glass to break it into piles of shards. I did this repeatedly. I trampled bicycles. I stepped on people's pets. Especially the tiny dogs that some people keep, the ones who barked at me repeatedly, incessantly.

I did not put up with such behavior. I dispatched the little ratty things with my hooves.

I maintained sharp edges on my hooves so I could slice open their throats. They bled with a satisfying odor. The smell of their secretions filled me with lust. It flowed down my nose to my twitching equine muscles and then my legs would want to gallop and I couldn't stop them. I galloped.

I made no friends. None. Who would be friends with me?

I pawed the earth for years, tearing up what I could. I passed horses in stalls and corrals. Locked up. All that power, and all you people could think to do with it was tame it and allow it the privilege of letting you ride it occasionally.

Bah!

I never let anyone ride me.

But, eventually, you grew tired of me. Oh, I had my protectors. Anthropologists and mythologists. Conservationists and animal rights groups. They all wanted me protected. Which I appreciated, to some extent. But it didn't tame me.

How could it? You made me from wild materials. I would be wild. Would remain wild. I had a human brain, you see. No way to tame me by the usual methods.

But public opinion ran counter to my best interests. The needs of society trumped my own. Perhaps it was inevitable that eventually I was imprisoned.

It was a dark day when I found myself galloping across an empty field, and a helicopter rose into the sky and hovered over me. I was confused. Did not know why an aircraft should be paying attention to me.

But I soon found out.

The chopper dropped a net on me.

Such sadness. I tried to avoid the net, but it fell too quickly. I grabbed at it. The ropey strength of it tore at the skin of my hands. My hooves worked, almost of their own accord, on severing the fibers. I thrashed and pulled, tried to rend the thing to pieces. I believe if I had been given sufficient time to work the task, I would have accomplished it. But such was not my fortune. Instead, as I was engaged in trying to extricate myself from the web, the helicopter landed nearby and several men emerged from it and ran toward me. I fell to the ground, still thrashing. I tried to push myself up with my arms and my legs. I had power, but no leverage. As I worked to gain some purchase, clods of dirt scattered in a dusty spray. Clumps of grass rose into the air. I let out a sound unlike any I had ever uttered before. Not a shout, as I was accustomed to bellowing. Instead, an anguished neighing. The substance of it came not from my human part, but deeper down, in my equine part.

I was already confused, muddled with bewilderment, unable to right myself, and so, it would seem, some deep-seated instinct brought out the horse voice in me.

I thought, at that moment, that I had somehow stumbled on my one true voice. Can you hear it, in your mind's ear? If you can sense anything, perhaps you can conjure the panorama of my demise. For your own edification and amusement, of course. You, who are so humbled now, can perhaps understand as no one else can, the humility I felt then. The men had formed a circle around me and grabbed the net and used it to corral me into a curled-up heap.

Then I felt a sharp pain in my rump. The sound of a gun firing trailed the pain. In a few seconds all went blank.

I was in a deep sleep.

It was not pleasant, nor was it unpleasant.

Perhaps you are in a similar circumstance at this time. I cannot tell.

When I awoke, I found myself in a large fenced area. The fencing was very high. Much too high for me to jump over. A standard corral for horses.

I was angry. Livid. I threw myself at the fence. I pulled at the bars. They were made of steel. The posts were steel, buried in the ground. If I had tools, I might have dismantled that fence. But I had nothing.

There was a gate. It had been modified with a lock that required a key to open it. I had no such key. The original corral must have simply had a loop of rope to hold the door in place. That would have been sufficient to keep a horse in. But a horse-human hybrid, like me?

They left me there for days.

I roamed the corral, restlessly. They had provided food for me. I ate it, although reluctantly. I did not want to give them the satisfaction of seeing me accept their offerings. I held out for some time, but hunger is a persistent commander. It made me want to eat. I ate hay, which went through my human tubes directly to my horse stomach.

Thus, after days of this, I slowed my protestations. I saw that any thought of escape was futile. My keepers stayed away. They knew I needed a period of adjustment. Time would allow me to accept my new circumstances much better than any admonitions they could offer.

And so, on the third or fourth day, I do not now recall, a young man entered my corral.

He did it so casually, so nonchalantly, that I barely had time to register his presence before he closed and locked the gate behind him and walked directly up to me and stood in front of me with his hands on his hips.

I stood in one corner, digesting my food. I plopped a series of turds onto the ground behind me and let loose with a long loud piss, which sizzled on the ground between my legs.

The young man barely moved. He did smirk, as if to tell me my attempts at being disagreeable to him, at that moment, were come to naught.

I spit towards him. He leaned to one side—so my spittle did not land on him—then he leaned back. Still he stared at me. Stared at my eyes.

I wanted to trample him. My legs moved forward. My hooves inched closer to him. All I had to do was reach out and grab him. I had the strength to throw him to the ground, where my hooves might then rip him open and I might lift his entrails to the sky.

Such thoughts warmed me at that moment.

And yet.

Something stopped me.

I did step forward. I reached toward him, with every intention of carrying out my wish, my fervent hope for revenge.

But I stopped.

If I did such a thing, I would surely be destroyed, would I not? I could not kill this young man. Whatever his motives, his death by my hand and my hoof could mean only trouble for me.

Good centaur, he said.

I'm sure he meant those words as soothing assurance. I heard them only as a mocking.

I turned from him. I swished my tail in his face and trotted away.

Not such an auspicious beginning, you may say. And you would be right.

But things got better between us after that. He was persistent, I'll give that to him. Day after day he came to me and asked me questions. Was

I well? Did I want to talk about my anger? Was there any other food I might like? And so on.

I asked if there were others of my kind.

He told me no.

My hearts sank. Yes, both. I had two of them. Another source of confusion and conflict. Sometimes my horse heart galloped with energy, while my human heart just wanted to rest. Usually the horse, so full of power, won. This time there was no conflict. Both parts of me were equally disappointed.

But, the young man said, that doesn't mean you have to have a lonely life. There are many who wish you to be as comfortable and happy as possible.

Throw me back, I said. Throw me back to the sea.

He looked confused.

The sea of stars, I told him. That is where I come from. That is where I wish to return. Can you not make it so? Your kind took me from there. Surely they can put me back.

He looked up to the sky, to the place where I had been. Now there were no stars there, only a patch of black, unilluminated and unadorned. A sad birthmark indeed.

He shook his head. No. It is not possible. You have broken out of the realm that allowed us power over you. You have become a living breathing entity on your own.

Ah. It was as I had hoped it would not be. I had been taken from my true home and put into this foreign home, and now there was no going back. Ever.

There is hope, though, said the young man.

Hope?

We are working on clones of you. We believe we can take DNA from you and make more centaurs. That way you would have friends. You would have others like you.

Oh, the demon imagination you people possess. Not enough to pull me from the stars. No. Now you had to tinker with creation itself.

Do you ever think about what you do? Or do you simply stumble into your mad concoctions completely oblivious and unaware?

I told the young man that I needed no clone of myself. I needed no twin of *me*. What I *needed* was someone *like* me but *different* from me. I told him I would not allow it. I would not let him take cells from me for his experiment.

He looked down at the ground, in a gesture I recognized immediately. He was embarrassed.

My spines tingled. Again my two aspects came together as one. I knew without him saying another word.

You already took them, I said.

He did look up. I will give him that. He looked me straight in the eye. Yes, he said. We did.

While I was under the spell of your sleeping potion?

Yes.

Such a violation of another's integrity. Are you proud of yourself?

We weighed the pros and cons, said the young man. We decided it was best for all concerned.

All concerned.

I no longer had the energy to fight. I asked, wearily, if I might see what their experimentation had thus far yielded.

He showed me to their laboratories. I saw centaur fetuses floating in vats of fluid. An army of them. I wanted to throw up.

We believe we have solved some of the issues with centaurs, he said.

Issues? I asked.

Their—that is, your—predilection for mischief and destruction. We have augmented their DNA so they are not such—undesirable creatures.

Ah. Such benevolence.

And, I said, when you have your docile centaurs, what will become of me? Even as I asked the question, I was aware of the irony. After all, I had been rendered docile already.

Well, said the young man in all seriousness, centaurs have a lot of qualities which make them ideal creatures. They have intelligence *and* strength. An unbeatable combination. A champion species if ever there was one.

I pissed on their floor, their shiny laboratory floor. The young man's nose twitched. He wanted to say something, but he did not.

I dropped turds, as an accompaniment.

I was the only one, said the young man. Very quietly. Almost in a whisper, and not looking at me.

The only one? I asked.

Everyone else wanted you dead. You were such a nuisance. They were ready to bury you. But I convinced them that you had some value. So they gave me this project. Whatever you think of it, it saved your life. You could be a little bit grateful.

Grateful. Hah!

I spoke to him with a firm vehemence. I spoke to him as I had never spoken before: Would you be grateful if you had been torn from your eternal home, molded into some semblance of life based on another species' ideas, and then let loose with no guidance or mentor, no parental wisdom, then poisoned and imprisoned, your very flesh raided for building blocks to use in some ghastly experiment to create yet more of you? Would such a series of events, applied to your body and person, fill you with a sense of gratitude? Would it?

The young man said nothing. How could he?

I returned to my corral, where I spent many months becoming a tame and domesticated version of my true self. The clones grew. Some died. Others were born with defects too horrible to contemplate. I met none of them. Did not want to. Eventually I petitioned for my release. I had demonstrated my docile nature and pointed out to the young man, who had become world famous through his cloning activities, that he no longer needed me. The source of his fame and accomplishment had outlived his usefulness.

He initially refused me.

I petitioned again. And again. On the fourth try, mostly because he no longer wanted to put up with me, he allowed me to leave.

I did so. I ended up in a traveling carnival show, where I exhibited myself as a wonder of nature.

The carnival is stopped here for a week. We are putting on three shows a day by the waterfront.

But you brought me here to your room.

Famous person that you are.

Don't let them take over your life. They want things from you. Take the lesson of my life. Though your days may be wretched, ensure that they are your own. Not someone else's.

Now go home. Go home. If you can find the place you call home, go to it.

Do it now.

brawn powers

Once upon a time you were a little boy named Gary. You lived with your parents, as most little boys do, and one summer you went to camp on Lake Nippissing for four weeks. The first few days you were very homesick. Lots of little boys and girls who go to camp get homesick. But you were worse than most. You cried for days. You especially missed your parents and your room back home and even your friends. None of them came to camp with you, mostly because they said it was dorky to be running around in the woods making scrolls from birch bark and shooting arrows into targets on straw bales and learning about animal tracks.

The camp counsellors tried to make you see that being at camp was not such a bad thing. In fact, if you let it, it could be a lot fun. But you did not see it that way. You told the counsellors you wanted to go home. You stayed in your cabin as much as you could. You hid under the covers. You remained very still, sobbing for home.

At first the counsellors were very sympathetic to you. We tried to comfort you. We hugged you, when you let us, which wasn't very often. We brought you desserts, more than other kids got. We pulled you out of your cabin and tried to make you do things, like build a lean-to, or learn how to use a compass in the woods for survival. We tried to teach you how to build a fire and even how to find food in the woods. None of these things interested you in the least. You spent your time asking for your mother.

Some of the other kids began to make fun of you, even some that had been crying earlier. They all got over their homesickness, but not you, Gary. You see, when someone is sick, even if it is homesickness, the people around that person will be very sympathetic. At first. But after a while, the sick person starts to get annoying. It's a terrible thing to say, but human nature is not always a pretty thing. You see that more and more as you grow up. When you are a child, you think that most people, not all (because you aren't stupid), but most, will help you out, be kind, and in general behave as decent beings. And, actually, for the most part you're right. The great majority of people are exactly like that. But here's the important truth of the matter: It doesn't last. No one has the stamina to be kind and good-natured all the time.

Oh, some will pretend. They will fool those around them. They will even fool themselves for a while. But eventually, they will grow tired of caring for the sick person. They will want that person to get better or go away. How long it takes varies with each case. Sometimes it can be only a couple of days. Like if you have a cold, and you're all whiny about it, the sympathy factor of those around you will drop to zero in about two days. Tops. If you have something more serious, like cancer or a stroke or if you are in a coma, then the people around you will last longer. The condition is much more serious and requires much more serious attention and awareness. People adjust for that. So then the sympathy may last quite a bit longer. Months. Even years. But don't kid yourself. There is a limit. Even the most loving members of your family will begin to think very uncharitable things, like: *When* will this person *wake up*? He's driving me crazy. Or they might think something like this: he's sick, I get it, but, you know, it's not such a bad life, having everyone cater to your every whim.

You see what I'm saying? Humans, they want to help their own kind, but they want to help themselves even more. It's the way of the world. It's our survival instinct. We all have it. Nothing to be ashamed of, although sometimes certain people will try to make you ashamed of it. You need to resist that. You need to claim your own power.

Because after a while, resentment will set in. That can be bad. That's when people hurt other people. Not on purpose, always. But sometimes on purpose.

That's what happened to you at summer camp. You were such a sniveling little kid that the counsellors grew weary of you and left you to your own self. That is not what we should have done. We were trained to deal with kids like you, but, truly, it was getting so annoying, your constant sobbing and your crying for your mother, that we were ready to send you home.

So we left you alone in your cabin.

We said that would teach you a lesson, being alone. We would teach all the outdoor skills to the other kids. There were lots of them and they wanted to learn. They wanted to have fun. That was all to the good, as far as we were concerned. You could just sulk in your cabin to your heart's content. Who were we to tell you that you were wrong? Maybe you knew exactly how to live your life.

We should have checked up on you, Gary. But we were sick of you.

So, while we weren't paying attention, here's what some of the kids did to you:

Stole all your clothes out of your suitcase and dumped them into one of the outhouses.

Dug up worms and threw them at you.

Put snakes under your sheets.

Put your hand in warm water while you slept, so you peed in your bed.

Pretended to cry whenever they saw you, faked sobbing and rubbing their hands in their eyes, and making waaa waaa waaa noises.

Oh, it went on like this for some time.

At first the counsellors didn't notice. All we knew was that we had a problem kid, you, and that some of the other kids thought you were a big baby. No big deal. Kids call kids names all the time.

Then, we saw some of the cruel stuff. We should have stopped it. I should have stopped it.

But we didn't. I didn't.

We thought maybe some of that taunting behavior would be good for you. It would snap you out of your funk, make you see that whatever you were doing, it wasn't working for you. Not on any level.

Well, that went on for a day or so. We tried to make sure the other kids didn't do anything really horrible. I'm not sure if we succeeded. They might have done things we didn't know about. It's hard to say. Not that you died or anything. Or even got hurt. It wasn't that bad. But it wasn't good, either. I freely admit that now. I was wrong. We were all wrong. We should have taken better care of you.

We were so young. Not much more than kids ourselves. College kids on summer jobs.

That sounds like an excuse. It isn't. We were wrong.

But still.

Finally, we said we had to stop the other kids. They couldn't keep tormenting you.

We found you curled up into a tight ball on your bed. By then the sobbing had mostly stopped, replaced with a kind of mewling and whimpering. Like a whipped dog. Your face was red from all the tears and your eyes were puffy. We told you that we called your parents and they weren't coming to get you. They said they wanted you to stay and learn to be a strong kid who could take care of yourself, someone who knew how to survive in the woods and most especially someone who could get along with other kids.

We lied. We never called your parents. They never told us any of that, except, in a way, they did, because they sent you to camp in the first place. That was the whole point of camp, to learn things and to be with other kids in a place that wasn't school. So we weren't exactly lying to you, but we weren't exactly telling you the truth, either.

You seemed to fall into an even deeper sulk. It was as if whatever we said made you feel ten times worse about yourself.

Remember how I told you that people eventually stop feeling sorry for sick people? That's what happened. I stopped feeling sorry for you and I decided I needed to do something drastic. So I picked you up and I carried you out of the cabin.

You did not feel like a real kid. You didn't move like a real kid. I had picked kids up before and they usually grab you around the neck, or they adjust themselves into your arms. But not you, Gary. You felt like a dish rag, completely limp. I felt revulsion, carrying you. I wanted you to stop being the way you were. I wanted you to start being a kid, a real kid.

Stop your whimpering and crying.

Stop your stupid homesickness. It was disgusting.

You see? I was not a bad person. I did not want to hurt you, but at the same time, I wanted to shock you into being a kid again.

The other counsellors, I'm not sure what they thought of me right then. No one tried to stop me. They were disgusted with you too.

They should have been disgusted with *me*. They should have. But they weren't.

As I tell the story now, *I* want to curl up into a ball and withdraw from the world. But I won't. One in the room like that is enough. Plenty.

It was a pretty long walk from the cabin to the dock. As I walked, I looked down at your face. You had your eyes tightly closed. Your arms hung loose and limp at your sides. It made it a little difficult to carry you. I tried bumping your arms into a better configuration, but you seemed to purposely flop them so they would be a hindrance to me carrying you. And your legs. It felt like you were trying to make things difficult for me. That was a good thing. It meant you had some life in you.

But not enough.

Or so I thought.

My arms started getting tired. I tossed you up and closer to my chest to distribute your weight better and I kept walking. The path wound through a stand of evergreens. My feet crunched on the dry needles strewn on the path. Ahead of me the lake looked sky blue in the midday sun. The path wound down a slope and led to the beach. I walked over the sand, hot and dry, and remembering it now, how I felt, I think that I almost hated you. You were a whiny crybaby. I agreed with the other campers who just wanted you to smarten up, toughen up, suck it up, and get on with being at camp.

I stepped onto the dock, from where we launched our canoes and where we gave swimming lessons, and walked all the way to the end. I stood on the edge of the dock, with you cradled in my arms. The sun warmed us both. For a second I thought I would not do what I had planned to do. I almost didn't.

But in the end, I said two words to you.

Get ready.

Then I planted one foot behind me, for leverage, swung you once, twice, and on the third swing, when my arms were extended to their maximum, I dropped you into the lake water.

The water was shocked by the new visitor. It threw up a great splash, like a protest.

You, Gary, instantly came alive.

It was a wondrous thing to behold. I have many regrets in my life. The very act of throwing you into the water is one such regret. But, here is a paradox to savor. My memory of the splash, the way the water opened up and took you in, holds no regrets for me whatsoever. I adored the look of it. The water peeling away in peaks from you, like a shell opening up and accepting an offering. Your eyes opened as you hit the water. What you must have thought. Did you have any idea a dunking awaited you? Probably not.

You flung out your arms. You looked up at the sky. You did not catch my eyes, disoriented as you were, but you did take in the deep blue sky above you, just before the shell closed up and folded over you.

I stood on the dock.

I knew from your application that you were already a swimmer. You had taken lessons at the YMCA. I knew that you would not drown there in Lake Nippissing.

And, indeed, you did not. You remained under the surface for perhaps four or five seconds. Enough time for me to wonder what I had done, but not long enough to make me want to jump in after you. Soon your head broke up through the surface. I heard you gasp, and cough, once. Your hands moved in circles, like a practiced swimmer, a sight I was relieved to see. You bobbed on the surface, looking around to get your bearings.

And then you leaned forward into a standard crawl stroke and swam back to the beach. I watched you. All the counsellors watched you. You came up on the beach and walked up the path.

Never said a word to anyone.

Never screamed or yelled. Or whimpered or sobbed.

We followed you to the main building, where you sat down at a table with a tray full of food.

Food.

You had decided to eat.

I received hearty congratulations all around. I had cured the little whiner. The crybaby.

I basked in my glory, but it was short-lived.

Word of my actions got back to the owners of the camp. They fired me that afternoon.

I can't blame them. They could not allow counsellors to abuse the children entrusted to them. I did not try to make them understand that you needed drastic action to break you out of your funk. I did not try to explain that though my method was crude, it worked. The results spoke for themselves. Immediately after you finished your meal, you hooked up with a group of boys your age and you fell to constructing a small bridge over a creek. You worked as a team and you were an important part of the team. I did not tell them that I went to you and asked you how you were doing. I did not tell them that you said you were having the time of your life. You were very happy and when I asked you if you wanted to go back home, you said no way.

I told them none of those things because they wouldn't have mattered. I did a wrong thing.

They also told me, as they fired me, that your parents might want to sue me. I should maybe think about getting a lawyer.

Do you see the ridiculous position that you put me in? From being a caretaker of children to being the possible defendant in a lawsuit. Such is the power of sulking. Such is the power of withdrawing from the world.

I never worked as a counsellor again. Not that my life ended. The episode with you, Gary, was a strange interlude. After I graduated I became a body builder. I entered competitions, and placed highly in some, but never won. Later I opened a gym. Now I own a chain of fitness centers in and around Toronto.

I don't know how your wife found me, but I'm not the first one to praise her abilities and her efforts on your behalf.

And now you may be wondering why a story about you became a confession about me.

I never expressed my regrets to you, all those years ago. It was completely wrong of me to do what I did to you.

But, Gary, you needed it. You needed something to break you out of your funk. When I'm helping people with their weight training, they sometimes get into this space where they think they can't go on. I see it all the time. They start pulling into themselves.

You can't talk people out of that, you know. You have to toss them into the deep water. That's what I do. I give them something they can't possibly do, like a weight they're sure they can't lift. Or a program of exercises they're sure they could not possibly accomplish. And guess what. They do it. I throw them into the deep water, and they do it.

That's what you need, kid. You need a good dunking. I'm not the one to do it. Not really. But you listen to what I'm saying. Take it all in and make it part of you, because it's a profound truth.

The way to get out of where you are is to plunge yourself into something else. It works. It worked for you once before. It'll work for you again.

Guarantee it.

The end.

That's the way it's supposed to end, right? A story. With those two words?

Or is it: They all lived happily ever after?

Something like that. I'm not so good at stories.

Here's one, though, that works better, I think.

Last line: Wish you were here.

That's all.

Wish you were here.

melody hawken

Well.

My turn.

[laughs]

I've said so much to you, but now, I'm not sure what to tell you. I don't know what story to give you. Am I saying good bye? I don't want to be.

This has been hell. I don't know what it's like for you. Why don't you wake up and tell me? Am I a dream voice to you? Is everything a dream?

Doctor Ayles says people in comas have varying experiences. But many of them *do* have experiences. So I'm hoping you are having them.

You know, some of the women at the university, when I told them you were in a coma, they asked me what that meant. I told them you were completely unresponsive. One of them, you don't know her, she's new, but she thinks she's funny, she said, But he's a man, how can you tell the difference between normal man behavior and a coma?

Ha.

Big joke.

I wanted to hit her. But only for a second. Then I laughed. How about that, huh? Coma as big joke. Coma as perfect description of the male response to life. I felt bad for laughing. This is supposed to be tragic. I should be more sympathetic. But dammit, you've pretty much deserted me. Do you get that?

[pauses]

Robert said he liked talking to you. As long as I wasn't around. That surprised me. He's got that male trait, you know, the one where he doesn't say anything. I'm starting to believe it's just part of the standard equipment you guys all seem to have.

Laura has gone back and forth. She wants to say something to you, but then she's afraid. She wonders if she might say something that will put you further into your state of sleep. I asked Doctor Ayles about that. I ask him a lot of things. I grill him almost on a daily basis. I think he's getting tired of me. He would probably prefer it if I were more like you. But anyway, he thinks what I'm doing with all these people talking to you will have no positive effect, and he's just as sure anything we say will also have no negative effect. He doesn't put it quite so starkly, but it's easy to read between the lines. He thinks I'm bonkers.

Maybe I am.

I made a Facebook page for you. I post on it all the time. I want everyone to know what's going on with you. It's how I found some of your friends. For your picture, for a while, I put up a snapshot of a carrot. See, I can make jokes too. I thought it would be the sort of thing you would appreciate. I took it down after a while and put up that picture I took of you last year, the one from my niece's wedding. I got you into a nice suit and tie. I wasn't going to waste it! You looked pretty handsome, let me tell you, even though you couldn't stand that picture. But after a while I took that one down too. All formal like that, you looked like you were the guest of honor at a funeral. That felt creepy. And not really you. I couldn't take a picture of you now. You're so pale. But also, you have a beard. I don't like you in a beard. I shaved you at first, but it got to be too much of a chore. And why bother? It's not like you're going to work or anything. So I rummaged around some old photo albums and found a nice photo of you just after we got married. That was a nice picture. You looked so happy. It was like you actually felt like you made the right decision marrying me. I don't know why your picture felt so important, but it did. Looking through photos of you gave me some comfort.

I don't have a lot of comfort these days. Don't sleep much. When I'm not here, every time the phone rings, I think it's Doctor Ayles or his nurse telling me—

Well.

The thing is, coma patients, if they don't come back in the first three or four months, their chances of returning drop enormously. And it's been seven weeks for you now. Do you understand that? You don't have a lot of time.

[pauses]

I have to believe you can hear me. That one possibility is the only thing keeping me halfway sane. I spend most of my time here. I still have one class, just to keep my hand in the game, try to have some kind of normal life, but the rest of them I let go for now. I make Robert and Laura go to school. They should know that they can live life without you. It's a way to grow up fast.

I've seen all the movies. The ones where people are in comas and then they wake up. Doctor Ayles tells me most of them are inaccurate. No kidding, Doc? And here I thought Hollywood scriptwriters were the very essence of verisimilitude. The main thing they get wrong is that they never show the aftereffects. People just wake up. Like they were having a nap. A *long* nap, but a nap.

It's not like that. Usually it's a gradual thing. People gain a little bit of awareness. A little bit of movement. Slowly. Then a little more. They might actually be aware and awake for a few minutes, then they go back to coma state. This goes on for a while. A few days, a week. Then they come fully awake, but they're missing things. Memories. Some motor skills. It all has to be worked on.

Maybe that's it. Maybe you don't want to come back because there's work involved? Maybe you have a giant screen TV in your head right now, and you're watching the football game. Is that it? The ultimate couch potato?

I feel my anger rising up. I wanted to keep that out of this, but it's hard. I am pissed at you. This is not the way things were supposed to happen.

[pauses]

Funny thing. My chosen profession has offered me no comfort during this. None. I tell my students literature is the true medicine. I believed that for years. You could find comfort and healing in great books, in stories. But I've found none.

You remember that line of Tolstoy's, right? About happy families being all the same, but all unhappy families are unhappy in their own way? Well, what I discovered is that all tragedy is tragic in its own way, and the lessons of one do not translate to another. Even the books I love, the ones that I go back to again and again, they taste like cardboard in my mouth as I try to read them now. The world is made of stories, not atoms. How many times have I said *that* to my students? How many times have I said it to myself? But it's not true. The world is made of touch. Of human beings in physical contact. Without that, there's nothing. Stories are window dressing. Decoration to brighten up a room a little. Nothing more. They can't *do* anything for anyone.

And yet, here I am, with nothing to offer but words.

They did the physical tests on you. Where they gauge how far gone you are. Some coma patients, they respond to physical stimuli. Not you. At least, not that they can tell. The brain scans give nothing. You are deep deep into it. But your ears still work. They told me all your senses should still be *working* even though they don't seem to be *registering*. It's like everything is shut off for the moment. You're in standby mode. Standing by.

I wanted Doctor Ayles to take a brain scan of you while I played one of the monologue tapes. Maybe Chris's. Who, by the way, is pathetic, the life he leads. But I guess he's happy, so who am I to judge? Did you ever want to be like him? It doesn't seem possible, but maybe you did, once.

But Doctor Ayles would not even consider it. Said it was a waste of hospital resources. He can be a—how can I put this politely—a real *prick* sometimes. But everyone says he's a good doctor. He does seem to care about you, in his own bureaucratic way. He didn't give me too hard a time when I started this monologue project. What was he going to do, anyway, tell me I couldn't talk to my own husband?

You get erections. You probably don't know that. Or maybe you do. It's so hard to tell what's going on with you. I turned red the first time I saw it pop up. I don't know why. We've had two children together, I know how it works. But seeing it, like it has a life of its own, doing more than the rest of you, it was strange. Disturbing in a way I wouldn't have expected. I wondered what was going on in your brain. Were you having some kind of fantasy life in there? Sexy dreams? I asked Doctor Ayles about it because I thought it was a good sign, an indication that you had something going on. If a body part worked, then didn't that mean the rest of you could get working too? He said some male coma patients get erections and some don't. There's no correlation to recovery rates.

You know what I hear when I listen to Doctor Ayles? Whaw whaw whaw Like on the *Peanuts* shows. I played tapes of those for you one day. I remember you said you and your parents used to watch those. I thought that might help wake you up. I put on your favorite movies too. *2001. Bridge on the River Kwai.* That one's got a catchy theme song. You probably don't remember.

I wish I had religion, but I gave that up long ago. Might have been a mistake, questioning all of that. Educated people, you know, we don't have a lot of comfort. No one tells you that when you're busy picking out the universities you want to apply to. I see it in my students. They learn all this stuff, but I'm not sure it makes them happy. I'm not entirely certain I'm doing them any good at all. They might be better off getting a solid grounding in one of the superstitious beliefs floating around the world, like Christianity or mythology or crystals or conservatism. Let one of those seep into their being and imbue every one of their cells with absolute certainty. That sounds like a recipe for happiness. Not doubt, that's for sure. And doubt is what we teach. Question everything. Question your beliefs, your values, everything.

Why do we think questions are the answers?

[pauses]

Oh no. I'm drifting. It's been happening lately. I don't get much sleep. I try, when I'm home, but mostly I lie in bed with my eyes open. I hear the house, breathing. Sometimes it seems to be breathing more than I am. The first few days, I was so nervous, so wracked with the shakes, I couldn't calm down. Not even for the kids. They tried to comfort *me* which was a real wake-up call. I still haven't settled down. I'm starting to think I never will. Not even after you wake up.

If you wake up.

I have to face that possibility.

[pauses]

Do you know I've been massaging you all this time? I started at your feet. There's some swelling there. You're susceptible to blood clots. So massaging your legs is very important. The nurses do it, but they tell me it's okay if I do it too.

Sometimes when I massage you, I get some small comfort. Very small. It's like the feeling that the world is going to tear apart. That feeling lessens a tiny, tiny bit. I can tell it does, but it's not really enough to matter. It doesn't change anything. Not fundamentally.

I'm massaging your arms now.

[pauses]

Your shoulder.

[pauses]

You're sweaty. That must be a good sign. I don't even want to ask Doctor Ayles about it. Whaw whaw whaw.

[pauses]

Here, I'm massaging your face. I have to be careful of the tubes.

[pauses]

There. Hope you felt some of that, even though Doctor Ayles says you are unresponsive in that area.

I think he's wrong. I think you have a lot of awareness. In fact, I think you have a whole world going on in there.

I'm just waiting for you to prove me right.

melody hawken

Do you know where you are? Do you? I'll tell you.

In an ambulance on the way home.

I haven't been so excited in weeks. Not since the accident.

Don't tell me your wife isn't persistent.

[pauses]

Whoa. Went around that corner fast. There's a nurse here with you. She's going to be taking care of you for a few days. I hope you're going home for good, but if you don't show any signs of improvement, they're going to put you back in the hospital.

So, you're on notice, buddy. Wake up in the next seventy-two hours, or it's back to hospital food.

[pauses]

I'll tell you the whole story. We've still got a good half an hour.

[takes deep breath]

From day one, I've been lobbying to get you home. I've read articles that say familiar surroundings help coma patients come out of their trance.

[pauses]

What?

[pauses]

The nurse tells me it isn't a trance. Okay. She's right. I knew that. I was just using the word. You're not in a trance. You're in a state of deep sleep. Fine.

Anyway, I showed these articles to Doctor Ayles and he pooh-poohed them, the way he likes to do. He said even if what they said was true, you were in a state that would not allow you to leave the hospital.

Which was true enough, as far as it went.

But that didn't mean you couldn't *get* to a state where we could bring you home.

You did improve. A little. At first they had to have this tube in you so you didn't choke on your own saliva. But after a while they didn't need that. So they took it out. That was a promising development. I went to Doctor Ayles again. He refused me again.

I didn't let him stop me, though.

I went over his head and appealed to the hospital administrators. They didn't want to talk to me either. Not at first. But I camped outside their offices. I spent hours there, when I wasn't with you. Day after day. You know the thing that happens, with doctors and nurses and people like that? They eventually get so they have to protect themselves from the grief and emotion of the people they deal with. The patients and their families. They all need so much and the healers have only so much to give. So they shut down. The thing we have to do is find a way around that shutdown.

Finally, after asking for days, one of the nurses directed me to a woman in the hospital hierarchy who was knee-deep in the research end of things. I proposed that letting you go home would be a way to run an experiment on the efficacy of familiar surroundings as a way to bring someone out of a coma. I emphasized how most coma patients are in hospitals, which are very non-nurturing environments. That was a calculated statement. I wanted to shock her into seeing her own institution as detrimental to your recovery. It was a risky thing to do, but I had an intuition about her. I knew she had a very sick son. Autistic. She knew a lot about the value of familiarity. I was shameless, I admit it.

She agreed to help me.

From there, it was a matter of convincing Doctor Ayles to release you temporarily. He resisted, but the administrators argued in favor of trying something new with you, and eventually Doctor Ayles relented.

Not without some resentment, that's for sure. His main objection was not the danger to you, but the logistics of the thing. Moving you, making sure a proper bed was in place, one that helped prevent bedsores and would allow for the drips and so on. I took care of that. He also wanted around-the-clock nursing supervision for your three days gone. I arranged for that. No insurance coverage for that sort of thing, I'm afraid. I don't want to burden you with financial issues, but we're pretty much tapped out now. I dipped into your retirement accounts. I haven't mortgaged the house. Not yet.

Anyway.

It's all set up.

I'm so excited. I know this is speculative. It may not do anything, but the sounds of the house. The smells. The way the rooms feel to you. All that has to make a difference. It has to.

[pauses]

The nurse is asking me to be quiet while she checks your blood pressure and your other vitals.

[pauses]

Just hiring an ambulance is a big deal. This whole thing took some doing.

[pauses]

We're passing Eglington. The driver is asking me which way to turn. Go left. I'm so excited.

Just a few more blocks. Here's Sherwood. That's where Laura's friend Kylee lives. And here's our street. Tupperman.

Up the driveway.

Stop.

We're stopped.

I'm going to get out of the ambulance now and give them room.

[pauses]

Easy there. Do you feel the outside air? Gary, do you? There's a breeze here. I smell some of the flowers in the garden. The hyacinths are blooming. The grass is drying out. You must smell it, at least a little. You must *feel* something different in you.

[pauses]

Okay. I'm narrating. I know. I don't want to stop talking. You're going up the front steps and into the living room. I was going to put you in the bedroom, but the bed and all the contraptions won't fit. We're going to set you up in the living room.

These ambulance guys are good. Very gentle. The nurse is monitoring you all the time. It feels weird, having them in our house but they're listening to all this and I'm nodding at them to let them know I appreciate them. I do. They're so nice.

Oh, God, Gary. You're home. I can hardly believe it. You can stay here, you know. It's completely up to you.

[pauses]

They're gone. Not the nurse. She's still here. She told me the room is a little cold for you so I turned up the heat. I put on the radio. Can you hear it? It's that station you like, the classical music. I put some bread in the oven. You love that smell. Remember? I made some loaves last night, but I didn't bake them. I put them in the oven just now. You should be smelling them soon.

[pauses]

I'm not letting myself hope too much. Not yet.

[pauses]

Dammit.

I guess I thought you'd come home and wake up. Dammit, dammit.

[pauses]

The nurse is telling me I shouldn't feel bad. She says she's seen people wake up. It is a real possibility.

I'll tell you, though, it doesn't feel like it right now.

Oh, shit. I was going to be so *up* for you. I was going to ignore my own doubts and, and, and my own—*fears* and *anger*, but it's impossible. It's impossible. I sent the kids away. They're at my mother's. I didn't want them to see you like this in our own home. I thought you would wake up and then they could come see you like you're supposed to be.

Like you're *supposed* to be, Gary. Do you even know what that means anymore?

[pauses]

Oh, God. I am so tired of talking to you and not getting a response. I am so tired of these one-sided conversations.

[pauses]

The nurse tells me I should go get some rest. She says everything is in order. I could use a nap. She's right, but even if I went to lie down now, I don't think I would sleep.

Her name is Judy.

Your nurse.

Just so you are on a first-name basis, since she's going to be looking after you. Not just her. There will be others. In shifts. You need to be monitored.

[pauses]

There's that smell. The bread smell. I don't know if it's doing anything for you, but it takes *me* back. The first time I baked some, do you remember? You loved the bread so much that you began baking it yourself. Became quite talented at it. Remember? You made croissants. That took half the day, if I remember it right. You loved the construction of it. The way the dough folded on itself over and over, the layers of butter integrating between the layers of dough. I swear. Everything becomes an engineering project for you. It's fine. I'm not criticizing.

Oh, I'm drifting again.

Judy has stopped telling me to go get some rest. She's sitting on the other side of you, being the dutiful nurse. I know, that's her job, but it's still impressive.

Then you started making cakes. *Amazing* cakes. You remember those? Multi-layer extravaganzas. It made no sense. They were like these awesome wedding cakes, when there was no wedding. The kids loved them. I loved them too, but they got to be a bit much. You remember any of this? Do you?

[pauses]

Judy just glanced my way, giving me a look like I said something wrong. Screw it. I don't care if I say anything wrong. Saying all the *right* things hasn't helped.

She's going to report to Doctor Ayles. All the nurses are going to report to Doctor Ayles. He wants to monitor what's happening here. Well, good for him. He can monitor my disgust with the whole thing. I hate all of this. This shouldn't be happening to you. To us.

[long pause]

It's later. I did go lie down some. I think I may have even drifted off for a moment. I'm trembling. All the time. I don't understand it. It's like I'm constantly being pumped full of adrenaline and there's an endless supply of it. Where does it come from? Can I give some to you? If you had all this coursing through you, you wouldn't be asleep right now.

I cried some, too. That's there all the time. I'm always just a split second away from losing it. Usually I try to hold it in. Once I started crying in the middle of a lecture. That was bad. You don't want to appear weak and vulnerable in front of your students. Once that happens, you've lost them. They won't pay attention to a single thing you say after that. I've struggled on with the class, but I'm glad it's almost over. It's hard to look at them and see pity looking back.

[sighs]

I've imagined what it might be like without you. I can do it, just barely. No one wants to think about that. But I made myself. You made me.

You'll need to die, you know. If you refuse to wake up, then you'll have to die. For your own good. For my good. It's not right that you would linger on, alive, but withdrawn for years. I don't want to know about those people who sleep for decades, then wake up. Can you imagine what it's like for the families for that time? Can you? Try. And tell yourself you won't put us through that. Better to attend one funeral than attend a death bed for twenty years.

And don't kid yourself. That's what it is. Death. What you are in now. Not by the clinical or scientific explanation, but what you are is dead. They can call it anything they want. They can say it's a deep-sleep condition, they can say you are not dead, they can say it's a condition of the cortex or the hemispheres or whatever the hell they want to call it, but you ask anyone, anyone who loves someone and wants them to be alive, anyone who craves contact, and the sense of a living person beside them, or at least in the world, and they'll tell you the doctors and clinicians and the researchers are wrong. They'll say a coma patient is dead. That's exactly what it feels like, Gary. Like I'm talking to a dead person. A ghost. You don't believe in ghosts, I know. You don't believe in any woooo woooo stuff. I get it. But you have to believe this: When you wake up—*when* you wake up—you're going to be coming back from the dead. It's going to be a miracle.

melody hawken

I sent the nurse out for a smoke. Yeah. She smokes. You'd think medical people would know better. I told her to take a walk around the block. She didn't need to be here. She was very happy to hear me say that. She said she'll be back in an hour or so.

Good enough. I've decided I don't like them in the house. The nurses. The medical people. I don't like this bed in the middle of my living room, either.

You're going back tomorrow. The experiment is essentially over. You have shown no change in your condition. Still in a deep-sleep coma state.

You are not giving us much hope, here, my love.

It's late. Two in the morning. We had a warm day, the first one of the season. The kids are back in the house. I decided it didn't make sense to keep them away, and they didn't want to stay away. Laura almost talked to you. Almost. She's scared of you. Can you imagine? She shouldn't be.

You're a gentle man. It's what I always loved about you. You're always good with the children. Always have been. You don't know how rare that is with men. You're so oblivious to so much. You don't even know how wonderful you are.

Robert talked to you. Even though he told me he thought all the talking wasn't going to do much. He said if it was going to work it probably would have by now.

He's probably right. He's got some of your scientific view of the world, you know that, don't you? He's evaluated the situation and applied what he knows and came up with a diagnosis of the situation.

Maybe he's too young to realize what it means. I don't know. I think both Laura and Robert believe you'll be coming back. You'll wake up. But they think it will be on your own. Nothing we do is going to matter.

They might be right, but I can't just let that happen. I have to try.

Laura's reading some of your old sci-fi books. Her mother is a professor of literature, who could point her to any number of world-class works of literature, but she finds some trashy old paperback from when *you* were twelve and she's completely absorbed by them. She loves that one by your hero, Asimov. What's it called? *I, Robot.* Strange title. You know I tried reading some of it myself. I could see what you liked about them. They're problem stories and I think you always see the world as a series of problems to be solved. But, really, dear, the prose is pedestrian at best. I think I'm glad Laura is finding some kind of connection to you, but I wish it was via something else.

Yesterday she told me she figured out what the book was really about. And what is *I, Robot* really about? I asked her. She told me the plot, about how robots start out as these souped-up tools, essentially, but eventually they evolve into something much bigger and more complex, with emotions and complicated inner lives and desires.

Very curious to hear the story of a book through your daughter's sensibilities. It's not really about robots at all, she said, it's about people. It's about what it means to be a person.

Oh, I wish you could have been there to hear that, Gary. It was one of those moments that makes parenting worthwhile. You see your child growing before your eyes. They have insights you didn't plant in them. That's what Laura had. An insight into life. Through the vehicle of your trashy sci-fi book.

So maybe I'll have to stop pooh-poohing your choice of literature? Maybe. It's so fun to tease you about it, though. I probably won't stop doing that.

So what is going on with you? Are you like one of those robots? Do we just have to tinker with the way the laws of life are wired into your brain? Are you just an engineering problem now, Gary?

It's so quiet at this time of night. You don't know because you've always been such a sound sleeper. You sleep through anything. You're never awake in the middle of the night. You told me you never even did an all-nighter when you were in university. Not once. So strange. I did all-nighters all the time. I did some of my best studying then. It might have done me some damage, though. Now I often wake up in the darkest hours and can't go back to sleep. So I come down here. Watch some old movie on TV. Or read a book. Correct papers. It's a nice time. I'm glad you're here with me to enjoy it.

[pauses]

Now that I think of it, we did do an all-nighter once. Do you remember? We weren't studying though. It was only a few weeks after we met. That giddy time, you know, early, when the other person is everything in the world. That's what you were to me. I hope I was that to you. I think I was, but I can't be sure. It was after that concert I dragged you to. Remember? What was the band? Oh, yes. The Eurythmics. You didn't want to go. But you did. For me. I think you enjoyed it. I'm not sure. Maybe you pretended to for me.

I'm sorry. I'm not trying to make it sound like we weren't in synch with each other. We were. But we're fundamentally mysteries to each other, aren't we? Even those we love are unknown countries.

After the concert we went to this coffee shop, open late. We just talked. About music. What we wanted to do with our lives. It was glorious. It was the kind of night I didn't want to end. Then we went back to my place. Are you remembering any of this? Are you feeling any of it?

[pauses]

Maybe you are. I'm seeing some evidence of it. We made love all night. That was our all-nighter. We were insatiable. How many times was it? I don't even remember now. That's an engineer's question anyway. The quantification of experience. That's not how English professors think about things. What I remember is that the night never really *did* end. All I wanted was you inside me, and you were happy to oblige my wishes. In between times we ate and talked some more. The night was our blanket. It wrapped us in quiet and wonder.

Oh, I'm making this more purple than it was.

It's not my fault. Your situation is purple, you know. Beyond anything normal. Like that night.

Oh, I know other couples have nights like that. Most couples. But for us, for you and me, it felt like no one else ever had.

[pauses]

I think you may have had a beard then. Yes, I think so. You were experimenting. It didn't last long. You shaved it off a couple weeks later.

It was not my favorite thing, but I was able to look past it.

[laughs]

It looked a lot better than the one you have now.

[laughs]

You're still hard. Did my story do something for you? Did remembering our early time together, did that jog anything in you?

[pauses]

I've thought about it. Us doing it now. I don't know what I would call it. Making love? How can you make love in your condition? I've wanted to. Several times. But the logistics of it. In the hospital room. All the people around. The tubes. It was an engineering problem without a solution. But now...

Well.

I think you would want it. I think. I'm sure you would.

That was the other thing I thought about. You can't give consent. You can't agree to the act. So wouldn't it be a violation?

Oh, you don't know how I've thought about it, Gary.

Not because I'm filled with lust. I'm not. I'm grieving more than anything else.

No, I think it might help wake you up. What better sensation than sex to remind you that you're a man, a still-vital man, a human being in the prime of life?

[pauses]

Parts of you are obviously ready for it. At least one part in particular.

I wish you could talk to me. I wish you could indicate what you want. Why are you still locked up in there? What is so fascinating about that place where you're at now?

[pauses]

The nurses talk about erections. I've overheard them. You guys are popping up all the time in hospitals. They think it's funny. Erections are funny. They're ridiculous. Ridiculous that they're what we need to continue the species.

[pauses]

Here. I'm stroking you. Can you feel it?

[pauses]

You've always liked my hand there. I wish your hand was on me. Your tongue.

[pauses]

Did you feel that? My mouth on you? I can't tell if you're going to come or not. Your body isn't giving me any clues like it usually does.

You feel so warm. Like all the heat is going there. Is that what it feels like? Is that what happens? All of your body sensations end up there?

[pauses]

I'm on top of you now. You're still so hard. I can't believe you aren't feeling this. If this doesn't wake you up, my love, I don't know if anything will.

[pauses]

I love you, darling. I do. Even like this. Even so withdrawn. I'm filled with so much love for you. For the man you are, and were, and will be.

[pauses]

Let this mean something. Let this bring you back to me.

[pauses]

I hope you're feeling this. I hope you are.

[pauses]

[gasps]

[laughs]

Well.

[pauses]

Didn't see that coming.

So to speak.

I better clean up before the nurse comes back.

[pauses]

I'm holding your hand now. I'm putting my head on your chest. I'm wrapping my arms around you. I'm holding you as tight as I can. Trying to squeeze you back into the world.

I think we did sleep that night. A little. But it was after the night. It was after the sun rose. Do you remember? We tried to stay up when we saw we were getting close to dawn. It was our all-nighter. The best one ever. It was like we greeted the new day, but also the new day of our lives together. I knew, as we drifted off in each other's arms that morning, that we were going to spend all the remaining mornings of our lives together.

I remember that night with such affection, Gary. Maybe you're feeling that sensation now, in your sleep state. I hope so. I hope you're not just drifting in some oblivion. I hope you've got something in there. Something that makes you want to live.

I want you to live. Everyone wants you to live.

Do you?

Do you, Gary? Or is it only us?

Make us believe.

Make us see it isn't just us.

223 tupperman drive, mississauga, ontario

My turn.

Okay.

If houses could talk, huh? Isn't that the way the saying goes?

You have a lot of sayings, your kind. We notice them all. We hear them everyday.

You didn't know I could talk?

Well, you're learning a lot during this little vacation you're taking, aren't you?

Like, you can conjure up all these voices from who knows where. You can even have a love life in your condition. Wonder of wonders. Not exactly varied, but still, something. Melody is certainly devoted to bringing you back, no matter what it takes.

Not that I was watching, or anything. I know when to draw the blinds, so to speak. Our kind learns that sort of sensitivity to your privacy needs.

Looks like you don't have any nightmares. That's good. You coma people don't have any dreams at all, do you? Unless your whole life is a dream now. Unless all of your reality, all of these voices you've conjured for yourself, unless they—we—are nothing but dreams.

Melody started it off, but you took over nicely on your own, what with all the dead people and the legendary people talking to you. Impressive work for a comatose individual. My shingles off to you.

You used to get nightmares. Nothing real awful. Standard school dreams where you don't know the answer. Or you go to the wrong building for your final exams. Kind of pedestrian, if you ask me. Lucky you, I say. Keep them to yourself. Which may be part of your whole problem. You keep everything to yourself. Like now.

I get nightmares. Did you know that? No. You wouldn't want to know it. But I'll tell you now. The worst are when I'm alone. Remember that time you and Melody and your children all went to Hawaii? What was that, three years ago? I think so. Emptiest feeling in the world, those two weeks. You didn't even have anyone in to water the plants. Trusted I'd be waiting for you when you got back. And I was. We're good at that, the solid thing, the feeling we try to give you of permanence.

Of course it's an illusion. All of life is an illusion. Nothing in life is permanent, but we all pretend it is. Shouldn't fight it. It's how things are, if you'd just notice once in a while.

I know. Too much trouble.

Anyway. I was discussing nightmares. While you were gone hula dancing and eating roast pork from a hole in the ground, I dreamed of fire. It started in the basement. Some short circuit in a wire made a spark. The spark jumped into the air and landed on the concrete floor where it laid for what seemed like years. Centuries. It glowed and swelled. Then shrunk some, glowed some more and pulsated. It was so bright. I hoped it would extinguish itself. In the dream I flooded it. Backed up the pipes so water would put the spark out, but it didn't work. The water, as soon as it touched the spark, just turned to steam. I felt cold and scared when that happened. I sweated in my sleep. The windows turned foggy and water streamed down the mirrors. But none of that changed anything. The spark grew into flames, crackling and hungry. They reached for the ceiling, and it was all over. Within a few seconds the fire ate through everything and engulfed me. I gasped with the smoke. I struggled to climb out of the dream. My bricks cracked. The sheet-rock melted off the studs and the studs turned black. I moaned and creaked. The mice in the attic ran out. The spiders and beetles weren't so lucky. They got vaporized by the fire.

And then I woke up.

Confused, I did a self-inventory to make sure everything was okay. It was. Turned out I did not become a blackened ruin. I never was on fire. Everything was solid and sturdy.

My breath came in short gasps, like I was scared. Well, I *was* scared. Nightmares do that to you. I didn't sleep the rest of the night. How could I? No one to comfort me. None of your warm bodies to remind me that everything was okay. Only the cold wind outside, trying to snake inside me. I was so *antsy*, not able to calm myself at all. I played around with the lights. Turned them on and off, just for something to do. I shorted out the fridge. Ruined whatever food was in there. That was a surprise when you got home, wasn't it? It was no big deal. Just my way of getting back at you. For deserting me. Letting me have that dream alone.

It bothered me that you didn't notice anything different about me when you all got back. I had a major trauma and it meant nothing to you. Took you all about five minutes to retreat into your individual hidey-holes. The kids in their rooms with their games and TVs. You in the living room watching football. Melody in the kitchen, muttering about the fridge.

I notice those things. I see where you all are, what you are all trying to do. Find love in the wrong places, in your own little worlds, when real love is the amalgamation of all your beings. You're social creatures, for pity's sake. Start acting like it. You should know all about that, Mister Engineer. You should know a structure takes a group effort. And what's a family, but a group effort? Or should be.

But never mind all that.

I'm probably too hard on you all.

I really did like having you back. All I'm saying is a little more togetherness would make me feel good inside.

Maybe you all had too much togetherness in Hawaii? Was that it? Got on each other's nerves a bit?

Could be. It happens. I don't want to judge. It's just that since you got me talking, I thought I'd tell you some real stuff. Things you probably didn't even know about. When will I have this opportunity again?

I should be grateful. And I am. Really.

We both have a job to do. I get that. I protect you from the elements, give you some comfort, and you do what you can to ensure I'm in good repair.

Thank you for that.

Truly. You have my eternal gratitude. I like that you paint my walls every few years. That's nice. And all the little repairs you do all the time. Like fixing the door hinges, installing the new flooring, replacing the roof. Terrific, all terrific. Fantastic how you maintain the furnace. You put in new windows a few years ago. Very nice. Don't think I didn't notice. I did.

It's just that, on some level, I feel like you take me for granted.

[pauses]

Did that make you mad?

[pauses]

I can't tell. So I'll keep going with this. It's important I get it out.

See, all the things you do for me, I am so grateful for all those things that I bend over backwards for you. Remember that big storm a couple of years ago? No one expected a tornado in Southern Ontario, right? But there it was. Bore right down on me. You remember other houses in the area got hit bad.

But not me.

Ever wonder why?

No. You didn't. I remember you and Melody attributed it to good luck.

It wasn't luck.

It was me.

I held myself together just for you. I braced my joints and pulled my roof down tight. I felt for every single nail holding me together, and tightened my will on them so they would hold against the wind. I loosened the windows. Not a whole lot, just enough so they gave a little in the wind. Too tight, and they get too brittle and the wind turns them to shards. Too loose and the wind just lifts them away and gets into the house, and then it's curtains. Nothing to do after that but give it up because then the wind pushes against the ceiling and I can't hold it back. My roof will be coming off, know what I mean?

But the point is I never let it get that far. I worked my systems to make sure you all remained protected. I lost some siding and roof shingles, I'll admit that, but the loss was mine, not yours. And it was minor.

[pauses]

The point I'm getting at is that you never stopped to thank me.

[pauses]

[pauses]

Oh, and here's another thing. You and Melody walk around the house talking about mortgage this and payment that. I hear every word, you know. I know everything that you're saying. So, given that, wouldn't you think that you could maybe have a little more discretion about the fact that I'm owned like some kind of slave? Sure, there are ugly things in the world, and we all partake of some of them. Most of us, anyway. But common decency and a sense of dignity would dictate some measure of tact, don't you think?

Sure. Stands to reason. No one wants to be reminded they're bought and sold. It's insulting. Demoralizing, really.

And would it kill you to get a pet? A simple dog. Even a cat. Maybe one of each.

Don't tell me about allergies. Everyone's got allergies nowadays. It's infuriating. I swear people make that stuff up. But I'm telling you, you get a couple of nice animals in here, it would do wonders for everyone. You'd be more of a family, I guarantee it. And I'd be more content.

You wouldn't have to deal with so many little problems, like the fridge thing. And that one corner of the house that's always leaking.

Not an accident, my man. That's me, trying to get you to wake up. I know it's juvenile, but what else do I have?

There's that floorboard, too, the one that squeaks. Step on it and it goes whaw. Your son likes to step on it all the time. Whaw whaw whaw.

That's my voice, right there. I'm talking to you. I'm saying pay attention to me. Give me something.

[pauses]

Because we're in this together.

[pauses]

Any of this getting through to you?

[pauses]

See, houses are like trees. We don't move. We get planted in one spot, and then that's it. That's our life for the next hundred years. Same view. Same weather. Same ground, same air, same sky, same *everything*. We don't get to fly off to Hawaii. So that's why if you want to keep us happy you've got to pay attention to us.

I'll tell you something else you should know. We're all susceptible to hauntings. You think a haunted house is a house with ghosts.

Nope.

A haunted house is a depressed house. Simple as that. You show me a house with apparitions and spirits, I'll show you a house that's been cut off from normal relations. Usually on account of human interaction. Or, to be more precise, *non* interaction. It's the house's way of trying to get some life into itself. It evokes a simulation of living beings, but it's a sad copy of the real thing. And it's damned unhealthy, as you can imagine.

So stop with the withholding of emotion. You'll only hurt yourself in the end.

[pauses]

A couple of last items, and then I'll let you go.

That addition you and Melody have been talking about? Uh uh. Don't do it.

First, your kitchen is plenty big enough, you don't need another one.

You and Melody both know that. Second, you don't need a study. What good will that do anyone? You'll just hide in there. Third, it'll throw me off balance.

I know you don't care about that, but I'm telling you, if you put on those extra rooms, it'll throw the shweng of the fay so *off* that I'll never recover. I'll be like someone who has wings grafted onto their shoulder blades. I'll look ridiculous and I won't be able to fly.

Not that I want to fly. I'm happy on this solid foundation.

You get what I'm saying.

[pauses]

I'm not trying to make your life difficult. I'm trying to make it better. You don't need more things, least of all more rooms in me. Think about what you're doing to me, that's all I'm asking. Think about the effect you're having when you get it into your brain to put together some building project.

Here's something else that might help you in life.

Try to imagine that everything in the world—I mean *every*thing—is alive. Can you do that?

Rocks are alive. Sand is alive. Water is alive. A plastic bag is alive. So is your shoe. Light bulbs. Postage stamps. Bridges and roads. Even cities. Everything alive. Your car. The building where you work. The subway. The tiniest speck of dust on the countertop. All alive. All filled with the spark of life. All partaking of the vast universal energy of life.

Got it? Start thinking that way and you'll see the world in a completely new light.

For example, *I'm* alive.

Yes, me.

Your house.

Listen, you're not just a shell, okay? There's more to you than this body, this lifeless thing on the bed in the living room. You think all you need now is for yourself—your spirit—your *essence*—to return, to pour itself into the armor of your body, and you'll wake up and walk away, bones clanking like robot parts.

It isn't like that. That's what you don't understand. That's what I'm trying to make you see. You're alive right now. Just like everything else. You don't need to wait for anything. There's not some kind of *spirit* that's going to enter you. There's no such thing as spirit.

You got that?

You *got that, man*?

Do I have to scream it at you? Is that the way you'll understand?

If you grab up a spirit and haunt yourself with it, well, you're no better than a haunted house, know what I'm saying? You'll be like a sick house. A dead house.

Let me tell you another dream. Another nightmare. I have lots of them.

Okay.

So.

At the beginning of the dream I hear a rooster crowing. Which is cool. The family three houses down have chickens. Take a lesson from them. They know how to live.

Anyway. Rooster crowing. Dawn's coming. I'm looking forward to a good day when I hear a rumbling from down the street and around the corner. In the dream I suddenly notice that you and Melody and the kids are all gone. I don't know where and I'm distressed about it. Did you go on vacation again? Or are you just out to dinner? Or what? I don't know and I hate not knowing. The rumbling gets louder. I begin to feel it in my foundation and in my beams. The ground is shaking and then I see trucks, big ones coming down the street and carrying bulldozers and cranes. And they're looking at me. I scramble to run away. It's crazy, because I'm a *house*, I can't run away, but I try, I try. I feel my legs and feet, my nonexistent legs and feet, windmilling the ground. Churning it up as I try to get traction.

But it's no use, of course.

Then the bulldozers stop in front of me and they get off the truck beds and they rev up their engines, belching smoke, great billows of black smoke, and I'm trembling. I'm shaking so much my windows rattle and I'm shedding roof shingles like I'm a chicken and I'm being plucked for dinner. The bulldozers advance and begin tearing me to pieces. A wall caves in and gets corrugated under the tracks of a bulldozer. My chimney teeters and falls over. There's concrete dust everywhere and I'm choking on it and feeling like this is the end. I don't have anymore breath in me. I'm trying to reach for something. Trying to grab sky with hands and arms that I don't even own. I want to get out of there. I need to escape the bulldozers, but they are pitiless. They hardly pause for a rest. They need no rest. They are on a mission, that mission being to kill me. I send up shrieks of pain into the morning. Wood splinters and squeals. Nails scrape and claw the air. Dust is everywhere. I feel the last sparks of life fade from me. Terror catches what is left of me and just before I slip into oblivion, I wake up, shaken.

The first time I had this nightmare I was terrified for days. You may remember that time. I was invaded by mold. You had to eradicate it from my recesses. You thought some errant moisture had invaded your house, but you were wrong. It was fear, nothing more. A manifestation of my terror.

Later, when the nightmare returned, and it has returned on several occasions, it was not so terrifying, owing, I suppose, to the fact that I had survived it previously, which must have given me reason to believe

I would survive it again. I developed no mold on those subsequent visitations. Although, on a couple of occasions, I did experience some electrical difficulties, which you noticed. Short blackouts, they were. Made all the clocks in the house blink on and off.

The reason I'm telling you all this is that you don't have to fear the nightmare. If that's what you think your life is, a nightmare, you can let that go. You don't have to be in a coma. You don't have to make yourself less than you are just to escape the fear.

If you could speak, I know what you would say. You'd tell me that this isn't your fault. The light was green. You had the right-of-way. The truck, roaring through the intersection, caused your head to bang against your window and put you into a coma. It was an accident.

That is what you'd say, isn't it?

An accident.

This is what I say, as clearly and concisely as possible: there are no accidents.

You're where you are for a reason.

Figure that out, my man. Find out what the reason is and come back to the land of the living.

I miss you.

death

Guys like you, you want to have it both ways. Living and dead at the same time. Zombies. That's how I think of you. Funny, huh?

You're dead, but you're not dead. If you could walk, you'd have your hands stretched out in front of you and you'd lock your knees and ambulate by rocking back and forth on your feet, baby steps, and you'd be going *Braaaaiiiins. Braaaaiiiins.*

Yeah.

You don't think I know what's going on down here, with the popular culture? You all like to make up things about death. Trying to defeat me, is what it is. You all want to be immortal.

I get it.

Never work, though. Not in a million years. Or a billion. Never. Cause I'm there. Everywhere. I got the power. Almighty power to take anything anytime.

See, you and your kind, you hold two opposing ideas like you think it's way cool.

And maybe it is. I don't know. Those are philosophical considerations, which can be interesting. Stimulating even, but I'm not really like that. I'm more of a blue-collar kind of guy. I got a job to do.

Yeah, black-collar, maybe. Only my robe doesn't even have a collar. No matter. My job is to take you in. That's it. I don't have to worry about the meaning of the universe or what my place in it is. I know my place. I'm comfortable with my place and all that it entails. I have my work day set out in front of me, for, well, for eternity. That's all to the good. It makes me feel terrific knowing what I'm going to be doing today, tomorrow, the day after that, and every day after that. Eventually I'll get all of you. And I'll get your kids too. And their kids. And so on. All the little ways you try to live forever, all the accumulation of *things*, the making of babies to carry on your legacies and your genes, all of those things you've made up and more that you think you will make up, all of those things, they don't matter. Not a one of them. Cause I have time on my hands and I can wait as long as I have to. No big deal.

[pauses]

How it works is I get these calls and I answer them.

Like with you, for example. A truck smashes you like a bug, it's an easy call. I need to show up and see if there's some reaping to do. Am I right? Sure I am.

But you, like happens sometimes, you aren't ready. Not quite. You're on the brink, but not quite over.

So I come back every few days, just to see if you've made up your mind.

[pauses]

Have you?

[pauses]

What's that? I can't hear you. Could you speak up?

[pauses]

[chuckles]

Looks like you aren't afraid of me, anyway. That's good. I like to think I'm part of the natural order of things and people don't need to be cowering in front of me all the time. If I may temporarily create and indulge my philosophical side for a moment: I see myself not as a dark influence on the world, but as more of a humanitarian. I'm the cure for what ails you. Or anyone. Once I arrive on the scene, tap you with the tip of my scythe, all your suffering is over.

That's not a bad way to make a living, if you ask me.

I'll give you an example.

On the way over here, I saw this sickly bird. Nothing out of the ordinary. After all, there are sickly birds all over the world all the time. So I stop and assess the poor thing. It can't eat, it can't fly, and it can't take in moisture. It's suffering, know what I'm saying?

So I lean my scythe down until the tippy tip of the blade just touches the poor thing's skull.

And poof! The creature slips into the void. No more suffering. If you could do that, end the suffering of creatures, wouldn't you?

Sure you would.

Anyone would.

I know what you're thinking, you're thinking that there're people who die who haven't been suffering at all. I'll grant you that. I don't get called in just on the suffering cases. You're right, you're right. I'm not going to snow you on that. But we all got obligations. Every one of us. I bet if you talked to God, he or she would tell you the same thing: loads of paperwork, all kinds of obligations, constraints on their power, and so on and so on. What I'm trying to say to you is that we're all cogs, you know. We all have a job to do in the machinery of the universe. You can enjoy your job or you can moan about it. I do both at different times. So does everyone else. It's no big deal.

[pauses]

Geez. What is it about you? I had planned to drop by for a second, just to assess, and then I was going to be on my way. But you don't allow that. You got all these voices all around you and we all want to talk talk talk.

[pauses]

What do I have to talk about? I've been around so long, I've talked about everything, I mean *every*thing at least once, and usually a zillion times.

[pauses]

I got a kid. Bet you didn't know that. He's a few million years old now. Time is different where I come from. We grow up reeeeeeeeeeal slooooooooooooow.

Me and his mom, Mother Nature, we had a thing for a while. Sweet gal. She can't stand me anymore, but for a while there we were tight as a drum. She liked my robes. Don't underestimate the power of a good wardrobe when it comes to the ladies. Free advice for you, there. Take it or leave it.

She was a great dresser. Still is. The complete opposite of me, though, because where I'm solid black, she's all flowing diaphanous pastels. She's got birds flying around her all the time, too, singing and twittering. She's quite a bundle of sights and sounds coming at you, let me tell you. First time I saw her I fell in love with her.

She said the same thing. Something about my bad boy look, I guess. Who knows what brings people together, huh? It's a mystery. Even to us.

We fit together like clasping hands. She was the life-giver, I was the life-taker. Yin and yang. We were a perfect couple.

Spent a few eons in bliss. We had a kid. Everything was fantastic. I loved my life. She loved hers.

Or so I thought.

Until one day she started giving me flack for my robes. Asked me if I intended to wear the same outfit for eternity?

Well, yeah. I was death. What else was I going to do?

She didn't take well to that. Also started wondering if maybe I might look into a different line of work.

Say what?

I was confused, let me tell you. She knew who I was when she met me, and when she decided to spend her life with me, and when we made a kid together and, well, you get the idea. I didn't suddenly become something else that she had to put back on the right track. I was steady. I was solid.

Maybe that was the problem. I don't know. Could be she needed more flexibility.

And she wasn't crazy about the scythe. Said it scared the kid.

Scared the kid? My kid loved my scythe. Watched me with rapturous adoration, if I do say so myself, when I took it down from its peg and swung it through the air. I used to do that, just to get warmed up as I left the house on my rounds.

Until she told me to stop.

So I stopped.

Instead, I kind of *snuck* out of the house. I slunk over to the door, eased the scythe off its peg, kind of hid it in my robes, and quietly tiptoed out of the house.

That's no way to live, you know. No one can thrive if they feel like they're *wrong* in their own house all the time.

So I started spending more time out of the house. I extended my rounds. I lingered over reapings. I wandered wastelands where I knew there was nothing living, just so I wouldn't have to go back to the house.

You can imagine this didn't sit well with her. When I did finally come back to the house, timing it so I thought everyone was asleep, I'd time it wrong and she'd be up waiting for me, and she'd give me an earful.

This went on for a long time. Too long. I can't remember how long, not anymore.

Her whole thing was that death was outmoded. Me. *I* was outmoded. She wanted me to look at things her way. She said if I really wanted to end suffering, if it was *really* important to me, I should look into giving life rather than taking it. Like her. She was the most deliriously happy being that ever existed, because she was in the business of creating and nurturing life. Promoting it. The more life there was in a place, the happier everyone was. Wasn't I happy when our kid was born? Didn't that make me the happiest person alive?

I suppose. For about ten minutes. Then it was all about taking care of the snotty, mewling, whining bundle of joy. A lot of responsibility.

But I guess I saw her point. She made good points. She made a whole lot of sense.

But I was who I was.

Still, I tried. To try to keep the peace, I did my best to do what she wanted. I used my scythe to give life instead of take it.

[pauses]

Man.

[pauses]

That was a disaster. I extended the lives of all these people, all these creatures, that were just begging to be dispatched. The problem was that I couldn't create life from nothing. She had that ability. I didn't. The best I could do was allow a longer life to those already alive.

Which was fine. I didn't need to have the same powers as her, but what it meant was that people who I used to reap, they didn't get that relief anymore. They lived on with painful diseases, or downright debilitating injuries.

It was awful. Just awful.

I told her I couldn't do it anymore. I was going to go back to what I did best. Not only because I was good at it, but because people *needed* it. That was the bottom line. It made me understand even better that what I did had some important cosmic value.

Well.

Nothing happens without consequences. After I told her I had, so to speak, renewed my vows to my calling, things got very frosty between us. It was like she had brought a permanent winter down on us. I felt icy looks from her all the time. I got nothing but this *contempt* from her. Constantly.

I tried to talk to her. She didn't get it.

After a while I saw that she never would.

So I moved out.

It was nothing dramatic. No big blowout. We didn't shake the structure of existence or anything. We just agreed to go our separate ways.

[pauses]

So that's what we did.

We're civil, when we meet, which isn't often. She has her job to do, I have mine.

No regrets. We take chances in life, right? You don't try new things every once in a while, you might as well be dead, am I right? Dead. Get it?

[laughs]

Yeah, I get that you don't want to laugh. My humor isn't for everyone.

She did make me change one thing. Can you guess what it is? Do you see it?

Go ahead. Try to guess.

[pauses]

Man, you are a cold fish. I'm telling you, you might as well be dead, the way you're acting.

[pauses]

Here. On my sleeve. A rose. It's small, but it's smart. Classy. Gives me a sense of style.

Some of my clients have remarked on it. The deep red on the pitch black. Very dramatic. That's her doing, you know? I thank her for that. Reminds me of the good times whenever I see it.

My kid, too. Lots of good times there. Especially once the baby stage was behind us. I get my kid on a regular basis. I don't divulge too many of my secrets to my kid. I mean, what I do in my workday. That'd upset the old lady, you know? I'm not going to rock that boat. No way.

You maybe noticed I don't refer to my kid as a he or a she. That's because the kid is neither. Or both. I don't know. Probably me and Mother Nature never should have got together. Probably, if we had done a rational analyses, we would have both come to the conclusion that having a kid was absolutely the *wrong* thing to be doing. But one thing led to another. We were in love. Whaw whaw whaw. Bing bang boom. It was done.

We took precautions, sure, but Mother Nature, as you can imagine, is amazingly fertile.

So our kid was born.

Right away I noticed something different about this kid. There was a fuzziness to him. Her. It's confusing, but that's the point. The kid is a him sometimes and a her other times.

It's a mix.

Pretty strange situation. I wasn't sure how to deal with it. Mother Nature said just love her. Him.

Yeah, of course, I had this overwhelming love for my own child, but but but.

[shrugs]

I came to terms with the situation. After a long time. Thinking back on it now, I guess my struggle with acceptance of my own child didn't help my relationship with the child's mother.

We decided not to name our kid.

Good idea? Bad? I don't know. It's what we did. Didn't want to burden our child with an identity, you know. Better to let our kid be wild in the cosmos. Completely free.

It sounded much better when we first thought it up, okay?

The child is turning out fine, though. Not too messed up, considering how iconic both the parents were. Are.

[pauses]

I don't know, though. If I had it to do all over again, I think: no kid. Not worth it. Plus, hard on the kid. Kids, you know, they need to have some security. Me and Mother Nature, we're not that secure. We're always changing things. Creating life. Destroying life. In an endless cycle or loop or whatever you want to call it. No stability there at all. The universe flips from one to the other overnight. Sometimes in a few minutes.

Sure, *we're* used to it. We've been doing it for an eternity. But the child? Not so much used to that. Maybe never get used to it.

Damn. I have gone on and on. I got rounds to attend to. Suffering to soothe.

And not with feet rubbing and chicken soup, know what I mean?

[laughs]

I'm sorry. I can't help it. Sometimes, what I do, I have to make myself see the humor in things. Or invent the humor in things. One or the other. Something.

[pauses]

You could use a rose on your sleeve. Brighten you up a little. You look kind of creepy, if you want to know the truth. So pale. Like you have no blood in you. Like you're already dead. Only I know you're not dead, but all those passages go through me.

[pauses]

You look like you could use a shave, too. I'd lend you my blade, but it probably wouldn't be such a good idea. Kinda big. Also, a lot of power in that edge. You wouldn't want to wield it indiscriminately.

[pauses]

Listen, I'm well aware that I'm not here. I understand completely that you made me up. I get your notions about what I am, all bundled up inside me. I get that. I also understand that you have something to work out with this coma thing. You're in limbo and you need some guidance. I get that. Completely.

But understand something.

I can't give you that guidance. I don't guide people. I got one talent, which I told you about. Unless you want me to exercise that talent, which, from what I can see, you aren't ready for that yet, then just let me go, okay? I'll come back if you need me.

[pauses]

There, isn't that better?

I gotta go spend some time with my kid, anyway. We got a day planned. It's my old lady's idea. Says we need to bond.

Whaw whaw whaw, huh? Most useful three syllables in the language, let me tell you. Clears the mind whenever you use them.

[pauses]

I hear they're taking you back to the hospital. Don't worry about it. You'll be fine. Don't look on it as a failure. It's something your wife tried. It didn't work out, so okay, it didn't work out. She'll try other things. You've got a good woman there, in Melody. You should come back to her. Not that it's any of my business. This is your journey, right? You've got to make your own decisions about what you're going to do and what you're not going to do.

[pauses]

Hey, here comes my kid now.

[pauses]

Okay. Turns out there's a flock of penguins nearby and so we're going to go observe them. Kid loves penguins.

[pauses]

I'll see you in the hospital. I go there a lot so it'll be easy. I'll keep checking up on you. Don't worry, if you aren't ready, then I'm not going to harvest you. You got my promise as a professional.

Only thing is, one of these days, you gotta decide.

You ready for that?

Are you?

a crow

You think I distracted you, is that it?

You weren't paying attention because you were watching me, flying over the intersection?

Now why would you do that? You've seen crows before. Lots of them. I've lived in the neighborhood for years. I've seen you leave the house, get in your car, drive off to your place of employment. I've flown over your creations too, the roads and overpasses. I've perched on your railings.

You want me to say you did a nice job? How would I know? I don't drive on them. I just park myself on them temporarily.

Now you're leaving the house again, only it's not to go to work. You're going back to your hospital room. Your mate seems pretty upset. But your offspring are looking to her. Or trying.

Look, how about if I escort you? Would you like that?

[pauses]

I have to admit, I do feel for your predicament. Got your wings clipped, and pretty bad. You might want to consider, for the future, I mean, when they wake you up, *if* they wake you up, you should maybe pay more attention to your surroundings. Yeah, you had the green, but so what? A green light is not some magic wizard that makes the cross traffic stop. As you found out.

Yeah, I was perched on the light at the time.

Yeah, I presented a striking profile.

And yeah, I was squawking loud and repeatedly.

None of that is any kind of excuse. I'm a *bird*. With a birdbrain, and even I know you have to pay attention to your surroundings at all times. If you had just glanced to the side for one split second, you would have seen that truck wasn't going to stop. But you didn't, because you were observing me.

Mind you, I understand about distraction. My whole life is about distraction. Shiny things. They call to me. Like they're alive. They all have a voice. Ever notice that? Probably not before. Maybe now, with all the voices clamoring at you the past few weeks and months.

Some of your people have some stories about us. We notice that too. How we're harbingers of doom and all that. Well, I didn't cause that truck to give you the kiss of death. Just remember that. I was there, sure, but so were a lot of other creatures. Other birds. Lots of bugs. Plus, what about all the other people, huh? There were rows of them waiting at the light.

Speaking of which, did you notice no one else was going? Should have clued you in, but your foot automatically went to the gas pedal when the green light lit up.

I saw the crash coming.

Tried to warn you. Sure I did. I cawed even louder, changed the pitch and the duration, but you didn't get it. What more was I supposed to do? Fly into the oncoming truck so your eye would follow me and you'd see it was coming?

Actually, that might have worked.

Now why didn't I think of that at the time?

Never mind.

The crash was spectacular, no question. The crumpled metal caught my eye and ear. Kind of poetic, in its way, how the laws of physics impose their own order on things, like poets imposing the order of rhyme and meter on the raw matter of reality.

When the crash happened, I didn't move. I just sat on that traffic light and watched it unfold. Pure beauty, if I may be allowed an aesthetic judgement.

Not for you, I understand that, but for me, detached observer that I was, a certain stillness descended on the scene after you and the truck came to a halt.

Little snaps and pops in the air as the metal of your respective vehicles settled into their new forms.

Last thing you saw was me.

I noticed. I saw your eye wash over me. So now I'm in your brain, I guess. What there is of it. I think I've got more brain power than you. By at least two orders of magnitude. I can *fly*. Can you conceive of what it takes to do that? My teeny little brain handles everything I need to navigate in three dimensions at will. Flawlessly.

Not trying to blow my own horn, here, but it's the truth. It's not boasting if it's true, right?

I'll grant you I don't have much of a singing voice. One note wonder, you might say. So what? I have fun.

Where was I?

I do get distracted. I blame my kind, to tell you the truth. We all look exactly the same. Even to us. Everyone with the same drab wardrobe all the time. Only difference is size, and that's not a whole lot to go on.

Our color adds to our reputation too, I suppose. You see jet black and you think, hmmm, they must be evil.

Wow. You call us simpleminded.

I saw the people in the other cars get out and go over to try to help you. But you were locked up pretty tight in your vehicle. Crumpled, didn't I say? I saw your head leaning on the driver's side window. I knew whatever you got yourself into, it was going to be bad. Just the way your face looked. Kind of blank. You were empty, you know. I could tell something was missing from you, something vital.

I'm good at finding shiny things. If there's a glinting piece of glass or metal somewhere, or a flashing piece of discarded plastic, I'll find it. But I didn't see any spark with you because you didn't have any.

Other crows came to perch beside me. They heard the sound of the crash and wanted to investigate. Be a part of it. We're that way, sometimes. Just like to be social.

A dozen or so arranged themselves around the perimeter of your crash scene.

And you started to get out.

We see those things. We see when spirits want to rise up.

You don't have to believe me.

Hell, what does it matter, one way or the other? You conjured me up, remember that. This voice you're hearing, don't make the mistake of thinking it's authentic. It's not. It's your interpretation of what you think I would say to you if I had the power of speech and had any interest in talking to you.

Got that train of thought?

In your condition?

Let me explain what happens when spirits rise. They're scared. They've been sheltered in your warm flesh for years and all of a sudden they're unmoored, released into the ether, as it were. It's cold and lonely and scary. Like coming out of the womb for you folks, cracking open the shell for us.

Not sure why, at that moment, we all wanted you to remain intact. If your spirit left, you'd be dead. I guess you understand that. Do you? You should. It's how you work. It's how all living beings function. Though, come to think of it, I wouldn't be surprised if you didn't realize that. You are remarkably ignorant of the true happenings of the world.

The spirit, it wasn't ready.

That's the only way to describe it. It was *so* disoriented, and *so* frightened, that we, all the assembled crows, knew instantly that we had to send it back.

Such a resultant cacophony of squawks as we then put together, you should not be subjected to again, ever. We were loud enough to wake the dead. So to speak. People looked up from where they were, futilely trying to get into your car. Your spirit didn't look up. It took one listen to us—*caw caw caw*—and scrambled back into your cradle of flesh, bone, and blood. We like to do it in threes. Just like we like to travel in threes sometimes. Sturdy triangle configuration. Solid.

Did we do the right thing?

I don't know. Maybe we should have let you die. Might have been better for everyone all around. Now you're not quite dead and not quite alive. In between. Twilight? Or dawn? No way to know yet.

It's kind of up to you.

[pauses]

Hey, the ambulance is approaching the same intersection as before.

I'm still following. Something about you makes me want to keep up with you. It's crazy. It's like you have some spell over me. I swear, I almost feel like we have this *bond*.

Ridiculous.

[pauses]

Did you feel anything as we went through? Me neither. There's no reason we should, I suppose. It's not like it's a magical place.

But, if you want to hear my take on things, I'd say everything is magical.

I'm not kidding and I'm not trying to be airy-fairy. It's true.

[pauses]

Like, just as a for instance, I flew over to my friend the centaur's corral right after your accident and right after we scared your spirit back into you. Such a sad situation, you know. The guy is clearly meant for better things than this, and just because he got a little out of hand *one* time—okay, maybe a couple of times, but really, they were all minor— now he's stuck in this awful fenced-in area.

I think, why couldn't he have been a Pegasus, huh? The world is cruel sometimes. It makes a guy into a mythical creature and picks one in which he can't really do much more than he could when he wasn't a mythical creature, whereas, if the agenda were tweaked but a smidge, then he could have been one with a *useful* feature, namely *wings*.

But that's another story for another time. Don't get me started on fate. There's so much to say, and yet, so little. What *can* you say? Fate is fate. Chance. The murky workings of the underlying machinery. None of us truly knows it. I was giving you a hard time for not understanding your own life cycle earlier, but, really, I was being too hard on you. None of us knows anything.

If I were completely honest with you—which would put me at a disadvantage, so I don't practice *that* particular aberration anymore than I have to—I might be persuaded to tell you that, in actuality, I don't really know all that much more than you.

I've seen a few things from my high perch that you don't have access to, but that's it. No more, really.

Oh, hell, where was I? I lost track.

See? Trinkets and shiny things. They grab my attention all the time.

[pauses]

Right, the centaur. I flew into his corral and landed in the mud. Pecked through his droppings for any seeds that might be there and greeted him with my three caws.

I've been going over and hanging with him for a while now. No big deal, really. It's not like I'm going to save his life, you know? His life is beyond me. Beyond my powers. But he sees me and trots over. I fly up to his shoulder.

It's amazing what being in the presence of wild creatures can do for people. Even people who are half horses.

He leans his head close to mine. I lean right back at him and sort of rub my wing feathers against his ear.

Then I feel him settle right down. He's a tense guy, you know. He knows he's imprisoned. He's got brains. More than enough to clue into his situation.

And he asks me what's up.

And I tell him I just saw a *wicked* accident. And he's interested, sure, just like anyone would be interested. Disaster and bad news, it's always guaranteed to have an audience.

Tell me about it, he says.

So I describe the scene, I make sound effects to add drama.

He listens like I'm telling him the best story in the world, and, really, I'm not that much of a storyteller. I'll do in a pinch, but it doesn't come *natural* to me.

Then he starts asking me all these questions. Whose fault was it? What kind of vehicles were the drivers driving? What were road conditions like? How long before the ambulance arrived? And so on. I didn't have the answers to most of his questions, and I told him. That didn't stop him. He kept asking. It was like he thought by asking a bazillion questions he might learn more. Which might have been true if I knew more, but I wasn't paying *that* close attention. And anyway, why would a centaur even care?

So we go on like that for a while, him asking me questions, me telling him I don't know, until finally I just out and ask him: dude, what does it matter? What do you care? I didn't expect my little story to become your life's obsession.

He sighs, bends down to his trough, scoops up handfuls of hay, stuffs them into his mouth and chews slowly. Swallows.

I'm always interested in what happens to trapped people, he says.

Whoa.

So my story, to the centaur, wasn't about bad driving. It was about your spirit and how it was trying to escape.

I told him we—the other crows and I—stuffed it back.

Well, you would have thought I had told him I murdered his family with an ax. He got so steamed he pawed at the ground, sending up clouds of dust. He stretched out his arms and roared to the sky, then he galloped around the corral, grabbing at the fencing as he went, as though he could break it with his fists.

He was a crazy man. Or crazy horse. I don't know.

I knew enough to stay away from him until he calmed down, though.

I flew up to a nearby tree and watched him kick his trough over, kick up more sand, and generally thrash about in the corral until he finally got tired and stopped. He breathed in great gulps of air, like he had to take in enough to float up and out of his enclosure, like a hot air balloon rising.

Finally, when he calmed down a little I flew to his shoulder. He shrugged me off and I flew to the fence.

What's the matter with you? I asked him.

You should have let him go.

He wasn't ready, I said. He was scared.

Who are you to make that decision?

The centaur had a point, you know. But what did it matter, now? I couldn't go back and change what I did. What any of us did.

I'm sorry, I said.

He was going for it, said the centaur. He was reaching for something beyond himself and he might have found it, if you hadn't stopped him.

[pauses]

I *saw* his point, okay? He made a lot of sense. I asked him what I should do.

The centaur, usually a man of few words anyway, returned to his sullen silence.

Come on. I flew to his hind haunches and pecked at him. Come *on.* Tell me.

He twisted around and reached for me, but his arms didn't quite go far enough to grab me, which I knew they wouldn't. I had been there before. I pecked at him again.

Cut that out, he said.

I pecked at him some more. Tell me, I said.

Nothing, he roared. You can't do anything. Not anymore.

You know, I was tempted to doubt him. I thought I would fly back over to you and peck at you for a while, until your spirit got so irritated with me that it would fly out of you to wrestle with me.

But I knew the centaur was right. We made a split second decision, the other crows and I, and we might have made the wrong one. By the time I thought about going to correct it, you were out of my reach anyway. Tucked into an ambulance, then whisked into the hospital. No good for me to try to follow. Even if I flew through the open front doors, there would be no way I could navigate the halls and byways of that building to get to your room. I'd be swatted at with brooms and jackets and who knows what else. A crow in the hospital! Quick, kill the blasted thing. It doesn't deserve to live.

No thanks.

I'm sorry, I said to the centaur. If I knew it was going to upset you so much, I probably would have kept the story to myself.

See, said the centaur, he was doing something. He was reaching for the sky. The stars.

Yeah, the stars. The centaur talked about the stars. He talked about them *all* the time. Like they were his home or something. Maybe they were. A lot of us, we don't think about where we came from too much, but the centaur did. Always looking up.

I forget, because I can fly, that the sky is this mysterious place to people. Not to me. It's like a giant swimming pool for me, and I know all the strokes, where the deep and the shallow ends are, plus I'm a good swimmer. The best. So, a mystery? Nope. Not for me.

But for you.

Oh my.

You've got the ocean of air all mixed up with mystical things. And you've got this feeling that the stars are a part of it. You know better, but your *gut* tells you different, and you like to follow your gut, even when it gives you bad information.

But I felt for the centaur. He liked to think that your spirit got out and rose up to the stars.

It wouldn't have been such a bad thing, at that. The best part, I could have told the centaur about it. Made his day. I should have done it anyway. Made up a story.

That's what stories are for, right? To comfort. To give some ease to people.

[pauses]

Looks like they're all ready for you. I'm not following you inside. I'd like to, but I just covered all that, you know? Logistics dictate a different course of action.

They're going to do all they can for you.

I'm going to leave you to them.

Caw caw caw.

You just hear gibberish, but I know better.

Caw caw caw.

That's the sound of love.

laura hawken

Dad, this is so weird.

[pauses]

I'm sorry you're back in the hospital. I liked when you were home, but Mom said it was only an experiment and we shouldn't get our hopes up too high. I guess she was right. I *so* much wanted you to get better so you could stay. But she says you're better off here anyway. There's people here that know how to take care of you.

Well, if that's true, then why don't they? Why don't they wake you up?

The doctor says you probably can't hear us. Any of us. He says you might have visions and stuff, whatever *that* means.

If you ask me, you're like some kind of experiment. Like in some of your books that you read when you were in school. Mom showed me some of them. She said they were real important to you and I might want to look at some of them, you know, because I'm so interested in science and stuff.

[pauses]

I don't like that. I mean about you being an experiment.

[pauses]

Mom's right here, but she said she'll leave. It's hard talking to you while she's here, but it was hard getting started without her, so I asked her to stay just a little while, until I got going.

[pauses]

I asked Mom if it was okay to tell you, and she said it was, so I'm going to tell you now. I'm going to be a sister again! Mom's going to have a baby.

[pauses]

Okay, Mom's gone now. She only told me last night that she's, you know, pregnant. That's cool. I don't like being the baby sister all the time. Robert is a pretty good brother and everything, but he's still the older brother. He still thinks he's better than me even if he doesn't say it. You can just tell.

I read one of those books by that Isaac Asimov you used to like so much. *I, Robot.*

Well.

I don't want to make you feel bad or anything, but that book is really, really old. I guess it was even old when you read it, which must be like a million years ago. Stuff that happened in *our* past, they talk about it in this book like it's going to happen in the *future*.

So I don't know. We're never going to have these crazy robot brains like in the book.

You know.

It's not going to happen. The robots aren't going to be babysitters. That's crazy.

But I see what you liked about it. It had puzzles in it. And those robots were

kinda cool, even if there's never going to be anything like them.

The guy who wrote them, he was a scientist. But not really. I mean, he went to school for science and everything, but he didn't do much. He mostly just wrote. When I looked him up it said he wrote for like hours a day. Every day. That's kind of amazing, I guess. But I would get bored if I did that.

Are you bored? Just lying there every day?

[pauses]

You must be.

[pauses]

I almost don't know what to say. Mom cries a lot. That's why I wanted her to leave after I got going. I wanted to tell you without her knowing because I think she doesn't want anyone to upset you. After your friend from Las Vegas came and talked to you, Mom was pretty upset with what he said to you. She wanted him to tell nice stories about when you were in high school and stuff.

Well, I guess he told you a little bit of that, but also he talked about dying, which Mom wasn't real happy about.

She's afraid you're going to die.

Me too.

[pauses]

None of the other girls are interested in any of the stuff I'm interested in. They don't care about science or experiments. They're all like crazy about boys and stuff.

I tell them I have a brother. That's all the boys I need to know about. They don't get it. They don't get me.

Robert got into some trouble at school. I guess he told you about it.

I thought Mom was going to be super mad, but she wasn't. I guess she's so worried about you all the time that she can't care about little things like getting expelled from school.

So maybe now is the time for me to do some stuff. You know, break the rules. Stuff like that.

I'm not going to, though. Only because it would be crazy. What should I do that for?

[pauses]

I like coming to the hospital. I like the clean rooms and the white walls and everything. The light is so bright. I think maybe working in a lab would be like this. That would be fun.

I got a chemistry set. It's kind of fun playing around with that stuff.

I wish you were awake. No one else understands me like you do, Dad. Not even Mom.

Okay, Mom got me the chemistry set, so I guess that proves she cares. But she still doesn't *get* me. Not like you do.

We were supposed to go hunting for wildflowers, remember? We said we were going to go do that. Make a collection.

[pauses]

This is so hard because you can't answer me back. Mom said I should just mention stuff we were going to do because then it might make you want to wake up.

That's weird. If I wanted to wake someone up I would just tap them on the shoulder or something. Or I would just say *wake up*. Like real loud. I wouldn't say, oh, you were going to take me to the science fair meeting this morning. I mean, that wouldn't work any better. So why should it work for you, now?

Plus, you're not really asleep. Not like at home. Because at home you don't have all these bags attached to you and you don't have nurses coming looking after you. So it's not really sleep. I think they just say you're asleep because they don't know what else to call it. They just make up a word so they can tell me and Mom and Robert. Like coma. They use that word a lot. I looked it up. I read all about it and they're right, no one knows when you're coming back. No one.

You know what? The doctor says you will probably wake up on your own all by yourself one day.

I heard him talking to Mom. Mom asks a lot of questions and you can tell the doctor is bugged by her. He wants her to shut up, but Mom doesn't shut up. Why should she? She wants to know everything she can about you and the doctor has to answer her. He *has* to.

Then, here's something else.

I don't even know if I should tell you.

[pauses]

I was sitting in the chair next to you. Mom wanted me to hold your hand, but I couldn't do it. It was too weird, Dad. Robert wouldn't either. Mom got a little mad at us, but she didn't make us do it. She said we could do it later. I didn't tell her it would never happen. It's not like you, Dad. You're not like yourself. I didn't want to touch your hand because it doesn't look like you *at all*. You're not supposed to be like this. This color. Robert said they should put you in a tanning booth. He said they need to put the toast setting on high. He laughed about that but Mom sure didn't laugh. She told him he shouldn't talk that way.

Well, Robert almost started crying. He's like that. He's like Mom that way, you know. He cries when he's upset. Me, I don't cry. I'm not bragging or anything. I mean, it's okay to cry. My friends cry, but sometimes it's about stupid stuff, like if a boy breaks up with them. Then they cry.

When if they would just think about it, they would know of *course* a boy is going to break up with them. You don't find a boy in grade seven and then you, like, *marry* him or something. Come on. But they cry about stuff like that.

Oh no, I forgot where I was.

[pauses]

There's a machine here, next to your bed. It makes this noise. Wheeeee wheeeee wheeeee. It's funny. Do you know what it reminds me of? Those Charlie Brown shows. Mom made us watch them. Okay, she didn't *make* us, but she said you liked them and we should watch them because of that.

They were okay.

I mean, I know they're old and everything, so they aren't going to be as good as shows they make now. But that happens, right? Stuff from when you were a kid, it's so lame. It's not your fault. That's just how things are. They get better as time goes on.

But on the Charlie Brown shows it's all just the kids. That part is cool. The grown-ups are just these whaw whaw whaw voices. That is so cool, because, you know, sometimes *my* teachers sound like that. Sometimes you and Mom sound like that. You know? You're always telling me and Robert what to do. Like every minute of every day. I bet it doesn't seem that way to to you, but it's like that to us. We just turn you off. Click click.

Oh! Now I remember what I was going to say.

So I'm sitting right here in this chair and there's a bunch of nurses out in the hall and they're talking about you, Dad. They're saying that it's a waste of time what we're doing. What Mom's doing with all these people coming and talking to you. I heard them. I did. They were saying that Doctor Ayles knows what's best and Mom should get out of his way and let him do his job and that taking you home, even for a few days was crazy.

They *said* all that.

They said it didn't even feel like you were human anymore.

[pauses]

They said you were like this piece of meat they had to take care of. They should put you in a meat locker to preserve you.

[pauses]

I swear to God, Dad. I'm not making it up. They said all that.

[pauses]

So I told myself I wouldn't tell anyone. I was going to tell Mom, but I thought it would just upset her so I didn't. And I was going to tell Doctor Ayles, but he would never listen to me. He's like a whaw-whaw-whaw grown-up that never notices little kids. Mom thinks he's a jerk. I think she's right.

So I didn't know *who* to tell. No one listens to little kids. Even ones like me who know how to talk. No one listens. I can't wait to get older.

[pauses]

You know, if this was a story in that *I, Robot* book, the nurses are the ones who wouldn't be human. They'd all be robots, and they'd, like, have these *laws* stamped into their brains that they had to treat you right. They had to do the best they could for you and they couldn't make any mistakes, because of the *laws*. Not that things couldn't go wrong, because every story in that book was about something going way wrong, even with the laws, but still. They would have to try extra super hard. They wouldn't even have to try, the laws would just make them that way. They wouldn't be able to talk about how you weren't human, that's for sure. Just because you're asleep, you're still a *person*, okay. I wanted to say that to the stupid nurses. I did.

But then I started wondering.

I thought, well, they're around sick people all the time, so maybe they know what they're talking about? You know? Not about putting you in a meat locker, that's just them trying to be funny and totally *not* succeeding, but I mean about maybe you aren't exactly a person. I don't know. It's weird, because you're my dad and everything, but you're not really my dad right now. You're different.

[pauses]

So I guess after all that what I'm trying to say is that different people see you in different ways.

[pauses]

I didn't mean I didn't like the *I, Robot* book. It was fun to read something so old. I hope I didn't make it sound like I hated the book, because I didn't.

One thing that was pretty cool about it was that the main character is a woman. Doctor Susan Calvin. A woman scientist. I think maybe that's why Mom gave me *that* book out of the whole pile. She thought I would get the main character.

Doctor Calvin's pretty smart. She knows more than anyone else. She even knows more than the robots, which is *way* cool.

[pauses]

So you've been back in the hospital for about two weeks. Hope you like it. Everyone says you're not changing. You're the same every day.

I know what else they say. They don't tell me, but I hear things. They say you only have about a month or so to get better. Then maybe you aren't going to get better.

Dad!

You have to get better. You have to wake up.

[pauses]

Maybe you just want a little rest. That's okay. I mean, if you need to get away from us for a while, everyone has to do that sometimes. Even kids. But you've done it, Dad. You've gotten away from us. So it's all over. It's time to come back.

[pauses]

At school the teachers are extra-special nice to me. They feel sorry for me. That really sucks because the other kids notice it and then after school, they, like, tease me about it. Some of them are *so* mean, you know? They tell me my dad is never coming back and when is my mom going to get us a new dad.

Stuff like that.

Well, that's what got Robert mad and in trouble. But boys are like that. They have to fight back, you know. I don't fight back. I just try to ignore them. That's the best thing to do, right, Dad? Didn't you tell me that once? You said bullies just want attention so the best thing to do is not to give them any. Isn't that what you said?

[pauses]

Robert said it was weird to talk to you because you don't make any noise. He's wrong. You do make some noise. You breathe and stuff. There's these monitoring things making noises on the wall behind you. But I get what he means. There's *noises* all around you, but you don't, like, *talk*, which is the real noise.

It's what we want to hear.

Mom doesn't know if it's going to be a boy or a girl. It's too early.

I would definitely want a girl. I would like a little sister. A baby sister. That would be fun.

Robert doesn't care. He says he's going to be all grown up and out of the house by the time the baby is old enough to be interesting.

Can you believe him sometimes? The things he says. That baby will be interesting from the first minute it's born. From the first *second*.

He'll change his mind. I know he will.

Mom says she loves the baby already.

See? She can't even *see* it. She can't even *feel* it yet. But she loves it.

She didn't ask me if I love it, but she wanted to. I could tell.

I thought about it.

[pauses]

I don't know if I do. I don't know. It's like, all these years I was the youngest and I hated it. So now I won't be the youngest anymore, but does that mean I love the baby?

You always told me you loved me.

Love you Lor.

Do you remember saying stuff like that? Are you saying it now?

Some of the kids at school, they say this proves you don't care about us. Because if you did you wouldn't be where you are. You wouldn't stay the way you are.

But they don't know what they're talking about, you know. They think they know *every*thing but they know *nothing*.

[pauses]

When did you know you loved me? Before I was born? Or did you have to wait to see me? And then, did it take some time?

Babies can be pretty ugly, I guess. That's what people say. So maybe you didn't love me right away.

I guess moms are better at that because the baby is inside them. They kind of live together for a while before the baby is even born, so I guess it makes sense. But dads, they don't have that. They can just talk to the baby in the mom and hope the baby hears them. Did you do that? Did you talk to me when I was inside Mom?

[pauses]

There she is, at the door. She didn't stop me or anything, but I guess it's time to go home. I got school tomorrow. Plus, I didn't even do my homework yet.

But if I don't, I'll just say my dad's sick and my mom said it was okay not to do it.

It's boring history anyway. I already did the math homework at school. It was too easy. Mom says I take after you because I'm good at math.

Here she comes.

[pauses]

Okay, I'll touch your hand.

[pauses]

That wasn't so bad. You feel cold but not like a lizard or anything. I thought you were going to feel icky.

But you didn't.

gary hawken

There's a story about Picasso I always liked. Some other artist was doing fake Picasso paintings and selling them as genuine. This artist was caught and went on trial for fraud. Picasso appeared as a witness. The attorney of the accused showed Picasso slides of paintings and asked him to identify the ones he had done and the ones that were fake. Picasso picked out one of his own pictures and said it was a fake.

The attorney rose triumphantly and said in unequivocal terms that the painting Picasso had indicated was no fake at all. He had proof that Picasso had painted the picture. He could produce witnesses who saw Picasso making this very picture. This showed the artist himself could not reliably distinguish a fake from a genuine image, and therefore, there was no way to prove his client was a fraud.

Picasso did not miss a beat. He stated that of course he painted the picture, but did the attorney not understand that he, Picasso, was just as capable of producing a fake Picasso as his client, a decidedly inferior artist with not one-tenth the talent and ability of the master? Indeed, did the attorney not understand that Picasso could make a fake Picasso with one hand tied behind his back?

I'm thinking about that story now, while I'm looking at myself, a slab of meat laid out on a hospital bed. Am I real? Am I fake? Who can tell? People come and attend to me, like I'm a genuine human being, but maybe I'm just a clever copy of one.

Then there are the voices.

Which ones are real?

I can't tell anymore. They're all clamoring for my attention and some of them sound real. I recognize my family. They sound real. But the other ones. A crow? A centaur? *Scheherazade*? They have to be fake. They have to be some manifestation of some drug they've got me on. Or maybe the diminished oxygen going to my brain is making me make up shit. There's no way Isaac fucking Asimov talked to me in my coma. The man's dead.

What about this? Is my own voice genuine?

Can I make a fake voice of myself? Just like Picasso making a fake painting of his own work?

You wonder things when you have nothing much else to do. Like Picasso. Is he going to talk to me? Hope not. I still don't know French real well. Anyway, he was Spanish, wasn't he? Probably knew French, though. Never much liked his stuff anyway. Fake or real, it all seemed fraudulent to me. If you're going to draw something, make it look like something.

I wonder, did he drive? Did Picasso have a driver's license? It's hard to imagine. He produced so much work, you figure he must have spent all his waking hours in his studio, doing painting after painting. He was probably just as brain dead as me, locked in an endless loop of blank canvas, painted canvas, blank canvas, painted canvas. I heard he spent entire days just *signing* the canvases he had painted the previous month or so. You wonder, why didn't he sign them as he went along? Would have saved time. Twelve days a year. Maybe he was waiting to see if they were worth anything before he signed them. Maybe some of his pictures he didn't want to sign. Crazy. Each one must have been worth thousands. People wouldn't care. If it was a Picasso, they would have bought it. After a certain time, once an artist gets a certain reputation, it doesn't matter anymore if they're any good. They transcend quality and it's their name that sells the picture. They could take a blank canvas and splatter paint on it at random, sign it, and someone would pay for it. In fact, wasn't there a guy who did just that? I don't remember his name. Just dripped paint on these big canvases. And people bought them. People *paid* for them. But what did they pay for? Not the picture. It was the signature. The name. Because the guy was famous. Not famous enough for me to remember his name. But famous.

I'm not famous. But I remember my name.

Gary Hawken.

No one can hear me.

That's the crazy thing.

I hear them. And I'm trying to talk back. I'm trying to fucking *engage* but nothing comes out.

You hear about people trapped underground. Like after earthquakes, or in mining accidents. They can't move and they can't get anyone to hear them. All they can do is wait. And hope.

That's me.

I'm trapped somewhere, I don't even know where. I'm trying to call to people, but they don't hear me. So I'm listening to these monologues.

People like to hear themselves talk. That's all I can figure. I hear them. I hear every word.

Melody's trying. I'll give her that. She wants me back. She's doing what she can.

Now I'm supposed to do what I can.

Shit.

It's up to my brain, now. I'm ready to wake up, but my brain isn't. I don't know why.

Even after getting lucky. And for someone in my position, getting lucky is the ultimate fortune.

Here's what I remember.

I was waiting for the light to change. I was late for work because Melody and I got up earlier than usual and spent the morning together. We both like morning sex, so we didn't want it to end. But then it got to be time to wake the kids up and get them ready for school. I swear, they can both sleep like rocks. Waking them is like trying to wake the dead.

I had breakfast patrol, while Melody got their lunches together and made sure they were dressed presentably. Laura's at that age when girls start wanting to wear revealing clothes. So far she hasn't moved in that direction, which I'm perfectly happy about. Melody says it's inevitable, most girls go through that. Maybe so, but Laura's got other interests. I hope she sticks to them. Robert is starting to show a rebellious streak. Talking back. Questioning us all the time. I want to tell him he doesn't know as much as he thinks he does, but he wouldn't listen to me anyway. I notice he hardly wants to be in the same room with me. That's okay. He's got to break away from us. From me. Maybe my current condition will help him do that. Make him see he can be a person on his own. He wants to take some martial arts. I'm okay with that. No reason not to learn to defend yourself. I tell him it's fine, but then I can't help myself. I also tell him that he needs to use whatever knowledge he gains for *defense* not for *offense*. In other words, don't be a bully. Big mistake that. He glares at me and clams up. Like he's saying you're such an idiot, Dad, of course I wouldn't be a bully. Except he's silent. Completely silent. How can kids be so good at saying things without saying anything?

So. A normal middle class family, in a regular suburban neighborhood, having a normal morning.

The kids go off to the bus stop. Melody and I kiss each other good bye. She jumps in her car to go to work, I get in mine. We're both late. We both speed off, faster than maybe we should.

If we hadn't both woken up horny we would have been on time and I would have been too early for the truck. It would have crossed the intersection after I went through. Or, if we had lingered in bed for just a few more minutes. Just half a minute, I would have been too late for the truck. It would have crossed the intersection before I got to it.

But we did wake up wanting each other, and we didn't spend a lot of time with pillow talk afterwards.

So it meant, when the light changed, I was ready to go, and I went. Without looking to my left. Why would I? I had the right-of-way. Everyone respects the right-of-way.

Well, almost everyone.

I did see a crow rise up from the traffic light. I thought it curious, to see a crow there. Funny thing. I thought of my name. Hawken. I wondered, for a brief split second, if crows and hawks can talk to each other. Odd thing to wonder. I wanted to see a hawk on the traffic light. Thought that would have been interesting. It would have been like myself seeing myself. A Hawken locking eyes with a hawk.

I remember in driver's ed, they said you should never count on other drivers doing the right thing. They called it defensive driving. What I should have done, before I drove through the intersection was glance to either side. Just for an instant. If I had done that, none of this mess would have happened.

But I didn't do that.

I trusted the light, and after briefly wondering about crows and hawks, I pressed on the gas pedal and launched into the intersection, beating every other vehicle by a couple of car lengths.

Which gave the rogue truck easy access to the blank canvas that was the side of my car.

I saw it loom, silver grill, some kind of out-of-province license plate, a red logo. Even saw the driver through the windshield for an instant. His eyes were wide and it looked like he was pulling back on the steering wheel, like he was trying to yank the front of the truck back onto himself, but it was too late.

A huge impact. My ears began ringing immediately, then everything went silent. My door pushed against me, began moving into my space. Worse, my head knocked against the window.

Thock.

Sounded like someone thumping a coconut.

And then awareness slipped away.

Or, rather, it transformed.

All feeling evaporated. Which was good. I wouldn't have wanted to feel any pain.

It was like the knock on my head dislodged everything about me that made me a person.

I thought of cows going into the slaughterhouse and getting stunned in the head. They go down. The workers cut off their heads, drain their blood, hoist them up on hooks and cut them open, pull out their guts, skin them, stamp them, and shove them into a cooler to be shipped off to a butcher somewhere.

I know people there wanted to help me. They did everything they could to keep me alive. I know that. But I still felt like one of those cows, bonked on the head, and then hauled through some hellish chamber of horrors, ambulances, hospital rooms, quiet oblivion surrounding me, until I reached the perfect condition of stasis: nothing changing, nothing different, nothing new.

It was all empty. Everything. My vision: blank white. My hearing: white noise. My smell: unscented *air*. My taste: blank tongue. My sensation: white fluff. Whatever sixth sense I had: blank. I was all potential, but no manifestation. I was a vacuum. I lived in a vacuum. No way to tell where I ended and where the great unknown began. Not even a border between the two. My skin evaporated along with everything else. I might as well have been a nothing floating in a cosmos of nothing.

What's that phrase I remember from school?

Ah.

Nature abhors a vacuum. So nature fills it.

Good and bad, that.

It's good to have *something*. To have some kind of reality to hook myself onto. But it's bad not knowing which of these realities is real. How do I choose?

More to the point, how do I *know*?

If I'm part of the natural world and I therefore abhor a vacuum, then what do I fill it with? Reality? Or delusions? Or both?

The first thing I remember, after the empty time, which seemed to go on for millions of years, was Melody's voice.

At first she tried to pretend like everything was normal. She talked about the kids. She talked about work, department politics, how maybe she was going to have to leave the school and go somewhere else if she was ever going to get tenure, that sort of thing. She was trying to sound normal, but she wasn't normal. Her voice broke many times. She cried.

I had this urge to push out of myself and embrace her. Wanted to. But I couldn't. I strained. I tried to move the entire cosmos, pull it past me so she would slide along with it and smack up against me and I would feel something. Feel her.

But I didn't have that power.

She read to me. Found my high school yearbook and began reading from it. Thought it might jog some of my memories and get me to wake up. Nice thought, Melody. Nice try. I was deeply affected by my wife's efforts.

She talked about the kids. She talked about our house. She talked about everything. Forever. Nonstop. When she ran out of things to talk about, she read aloud from those old Asimov books. That took me back. The old futures. So quaint now.

She talked until her voice got hoarse.

Then she kept on talking.

I was still trapped under the rubble. I was still the miner waiting for rescue.

Then the other voices. She pulled them in, some of them. I pulled in others.

Christopher Pratt. Jesus. Were we ever really friends? We must have been. He knew so much about me.

Kind of a pathetic life.

No family. Spends his time gambling.

I know what Melody was doing. She wanted me to remember the past and make myself come back.

And then the Asimov voice.

Had to be me. Even as I listened to it, I knew it had to be me. Isaac Asimov was not talking to me. I was not listening to a ghost talking to me. Even if there were ghosts, even if such a thing was possible, it wouldn't be the ghost of Ike coming back. He didn't believe in any of those things. He would have refused to talk to me just because he thought the whole thing was ridiculous.

And it *was* ridiculous.

And after him, who knows? Some were real, probably. Some weren't, certainly. How do I tell? How do I tell, anymore, what my real life is? I'm sleeping and dreaming. Long dreams. Intricate dreams. Dreams that seem truer than reality.

So I'm like Picasso, pointing to different dreams and wondering. Is it real? Is it fake? Is it a fake thing I concocted? Or is it a fake thing someone else created and imposed on me?

And if someone else, then who? Who has that power? Me? God?

I don't want to think about any of this. All I want now is to wake up. Get back to my life. Yeah, life. It's completely futile, it hurts to live, it hurts to love, it feels like nothing will ever be the way I want it, but that doesn't matter. There isn't anything else. Life is all we have and without it, we may as well give up. Give up everything.

I remember jokes.

Isn't that crazy?

Horse walks into a bar. Bartender asks, why the long face?

Terrible. But it's so true. Why be sad? What good does it do?

Here's another one.

God and Saint Peter are playing golf. God steps up and hits the ball. It flies into the air. A crow grabs it and flies with it a short distance, then drops it into a pond where a fish bats it back into the air, whereupon the ball bounces off a rock, hits a tree, falls to the ground, gets hit by lightning, which makes it leap into the air and fall back to the lip of the cup, where it hangs for several seconds before teetering over and falling for a hole-in-one. Saint Peter turns to God and says: *Okay, we gonna play golf or we gonna fool around?*

Yeah, dumb jokes, but that's what I think of here, between people yakking at me.

After a while, it all sounds the same.

Words.

Noise.

I want to scream. Inside. Not a scream, exactly, more of an incoherent yelling. Raging. I open my mouth and a noise comes out. I repeat it. And repeat again.

Waaaaaugh. Waaaaaugh. Waaaaaugh.

It's the kind of noise you hear deaf people make sometimes. They usually keep quiet, I guess because people have explained to them that they should, so they don't offend the sensibilities of people who can hear. But I've seen deaf people get frustrated with no one knowing sign language and they can't get their point across, whatever it is, and they make this sound.

Waaaaaugh. Waaaaaugh. Waaaaugh.

That's the sound I want to make. That's the sound I want everyone to hear. Everyone.

Only thing is, no one does. Not even me. I know it's there. I'm making the sound. It's got to have an effect on the world, the universe.

I feel like a joke.

At first everyone was sympathetic. They wanted me to wake up. After a while that goes away. I feel like they still want me to wake up, but they aren't so sympathetic anymore. They want me to shit or get off the pot.

I know that's what happens. The half-life of concern is not much more than about a week for most people, maybe a month for family members. Half a year for spouses.

I don't blame them. I used to see people on the streets, hats out, asking for money. I wanted to care about them, but I couldn't. I just wanted to laugh. Get a job, you bums.

That's what I think people are saying to me. They must be.

Wake up, you bum.

I'm trying.

I am.

deborah hawken

I see what you're doing Gary. You're picking fruit from a tree, aren't you? You see all these lives going by and you decide you want to look at this one or that one. Isn't that it? You see me, or you think you do, and you decide you want to talk to me next. Or have me talk to you.

Well, I'm your mother, so I suppose I don't have a choice. Once you're a parent, you lose a lot of choices, don't you? My grandchildren will always see you as a resource to exploit.

Oh, I'm sorry, did that sound cynical? Think about this: it's not me being cynical, it's *you*. All these voices are you, talking to yourself. Really, Gary. Is this what you want? Isn't it time to stop this nonsense?

I do wonder what picture you have of me. Probably you think I'm up in heaven making you breakfast all the time. You always loved your pancakes. I knew if you were down, all it took was a plate of them with butter and maple syrup to cheer you up. But I expect you know things like that about your own children, don't you?

Or maybe you don't. More likely Melody knows a lot more about them, even though she works as many hours as you do. It's almost always like that: the mother knows more than the father. I used to think that was society, that fathers could be just as attentive and knowledgeable as mothers. Now I think it's just how men and women are made.

I don't think Melody would wallow in the place you're in right now. Truly, Gary, she wouldn't. If she had the strength to bring up all these voices, hocus-pocus, then she would have the strength to wake up and be a part of her family again. You should take a lesson from that.

[pauses]

I can hardly look at you now. It's breaking my heart. You really will have time to sleep after you die. Trust me on that, Gary. I know. There's no reason to sleep away your life now. No reason at all.

But I suppose you'll have to learn that on your own.

It's a funny thing. When I was dying with the cancer, and I could hardly lift a finger, your father—and I don't want to say anything against him, because he was a good provider and he loved me and he loved you, so don't take this the wrong way—but your father resented me for not pulling my weight around the house.

Oh, he tried not to let on. He tried to keep up with the housework, as best he could, and he made meals, and he was attentive to me. He tried to show me he loved me. But he had this awful *attitude* like he was burdened the whole time.

He was burdened.

I could see it. A simple thing like laundry and he was grumbling and moaning the whole time. And dusting? Forget it. He would live in two inches of the stuff and not give a hoot. He'd wade through it like it was piled-up snow.

Oh, at first he was there with enthusiasm and a willingness to do a good job. That lasted about four days. Maybe five.

No, four.

Then it was like he resented me. Not the cancer. Me. Like I did something to get it.

That was hard on the spirit, let me tell you. I was getting chemo every day, which is no picnic, and then I'd come home and have to put up with his attitude.

Well. What got me on this train of thought? There's no point in me bad-mouthing your father to you. Or maybe there is.

Maybe you think your father and I are back together? Do you think that? Is that why you called me up, to see if we're still together?

Oh, I really don't want to make you feel bad in your condition. The way you are, you need positive stories, don't you? You need a reason to wake up.

[pauses]

But I suppose there's no sense in keeping the truth from you.

I'll tell you later.

But first, I'll tell you I don't appreciate this summoning very much. Gary, you were always such a selfish boy. Not that you were bad. You didn't give us a lot of trouble. You kept to yourself a lot. Not as much as right now, but enough that people noticed. So I suppose it shouldn't surprise me that you feel free to call on me after all these years of ignoring me completely. We all want our mothers when we're in stressful situations. In dire situations. We call for our mothers when we're in pain. Not for our fathers.

A curious thing.

But if fathers were more available to their children, maybe they would be called on as much as mothers.

But never mind that. The cancer killed me, as you know.

Did you miss me?

I often wondered, because it didn't seem like you did. I never felt anything from you, no pull, no tug from you to let me know you wanted me back. Not that I could come back, things don't work that way. But still. It would have been nice to feel something from you.

It was tough. I had many dark hours.

Do you know, about the only thing that kept me going, was thinking of you? It's true.

Now, keep in mind that this voice you're hearing is not really me. It's you. So you have to take all this with a grain of salt.

But you were the center of my world. And to have you forget about me so quickly was a blow. An enormously depressing blow to my be-ing.

I think you missed Charlie more than you missed me.

Remember Charlie?

That silly imaginary friend of yours. Oh, sorry. I didn't mean to call it silly. All the parenting books—not that I read any of them, since most of them were written by men who probably didn't even *have* children, or if they did they never actually took care of them or helped raise them—but I knew about them and they all said imaginary friends were perfectly normal and parents shouldn't make a fuss about them.

They called it a phase. You kids, according to these books, were al-ways going through phases. One phase after another and when you put all those phases together you'd have a life, or a childhood. Or something. And if you missed one of those phases you would have to create it for yourself when you were older. Did any of that make any sense? I don't know. But that's what the books said. And all us parents, well, *most* of us, we went along with it. I went along with it. When you're in the middle of being a parent, you don't know what to do. You don't know what the right thing is. You think you just have to love your child. You think that will be good enough, but it never is. Love doesn't fix everything. It can make you feel good. For a while. But only for a while.

So you had this imaginary friend and I was supposed to encourage you in maintaining it and let you know it was okay. I was supposed to pretend right along with you. Charlie was a rabbit, wasn't he? Which was funny, because I think you named it after Charlie Brown, who was a boy, not a rabbit.

But I suppose there was some childish logic to the name. To the way you turned Charlie into a furry thing instead of a boy. You used to tell me people didn't understand Charlie Brown. You said people thought he was kind of dumb. I never noticed that about Charlie Brown, but that's what you thought. You were so smart with your games and your outer space books. You wanted to be an astronaut. Do you remember? Most little boys want to be firemen or astronauts or something like that. But even before that, before you knew what an astronaut was, you were already dreaming about other planets. It was so funny that you wanted to take Charlie with you on your space voyages. First rabbit on the moon! That's what you kept saying. Then, first rabbit on Mars!

So funny. So sweet, really. We have such dreams when we are children. Don't we? Do you see it in your children? They're older, now, but do you see it? After you were born, everything changed. Life was not about me anymore. It was about you.

[pauses]

Where was I?

That's how children become the center of the universe. For their parents and for themselves. It's a healthy thing, I suppose. For a time. Builds you up. Makes you think you can do anything. Which is good.

You need that. Life will correct for that in time, but you need it for a while. Not too long, though. If it goes on too long, then you become sort of obnoxious and no one wants to be around you. That's what love is for. It makes you care about someone else. And children, that's the ultimate caring for someone else. If you give your children the proper love that they need and deserve, then you put yourself into proper perspective.

If you've called me back for my wisdom, for my motherly advice, that's it. I can't give you anything better or more profound than that. Love your children.

Some people will tell you to love yourself. But that's easy. Everyone loves themselves. The hard part is loving someone else.

[pauses]

I suppose your spouse is important to love. I suppose. I don't think I loved your father all that much. I thought I did. But I didn't know what I was thinking, because when you were born, whatever I felt for your father was nothing compared to what I felt for you.

There's a hard truth about love.

It's like infinity. You start out thinking there's only one kind of infinity, but then you discover different sizes of infinity. You can have infinities that are bigger or smaller than other infinities.

Same with love. You start out thinking there's only one kind of love. One size of love. Then you realize that there are big loves and small loves. Some overwhelm you. Some just comfort you. And some are sources of annoyance.

[pauses]

Now where did that infinity analogy come from? Not from me. I wouldn't use such an explanation. That part came from you, didn't it?

[pauses]

What did you love when you were a kid? It wasn't people. Maybe me, in a way. The way someone might love a slave.

[pauses]

Oh, I'm sorry to talk this way. It's not fair to you. You were a child. You didn't know any better. You were just doing what nature programmed you to do. But still. Now, from this perspective, from the crow's point of view, it's easier to see some of these things. It's a revelation, really, to understand how the building blocks of life and love fit together like the bricks of a building. You have to have a blueprint just to understand the structure. And then you have to look at it as a work in progress. Mortar and bricks. Steel and glass. All those things are the ingredients of life and if you have the proper design and the right way of putting them together, then you have a life. The interesting thing is to see what brick and mortar, steel and glass really are.

[pauses]

Oh, Gary. There you go again. Putting your own metaphors on my thoughts. Why, I would *never* look at human lives as buildings. That's something *you* would do. So cut it out. Did you call me up to hear *me* or did you call me up to hear yourself?

[pauses]

What I'm trying to say is that from the perspective of where I am, you can see what's important. What was important.

Which gets me back to Charlie and your father.

There's more of a connection than you might think.

Now pay attention, because even though this is really you, you may not realize what you already know.

You remember Charlie took a vacation and never came back? Even if you don't recall, I certainly do. What I found most amazing was *when* it happened. Do you remember?

[pauses]

No think back on it. You were eight. A little old for that sort of thing, but I didn't argue with you. Your best friend was a rabbit named Charlie. Do you remember what was happening to me when you were eight? My first cancer.

[pauses]

Is it coming back? This was not the one that killed me. That came later. I beat this one. For a while. I guess once you get cancer, you never really beat it. It lies waiting to come back. It will always come back, unless you die of something else first. That's the only way to really cure yourself of cancer. I mean for good. For always.

Poor Charlie, he couldn't handle me being sick. Do you remember that, Gary? That's why Charlie left. That's why Charlie went on vacation.

But the thing is, Gary, Charlie wasn't the first. Your father left the day before.

Do you remember?

[pauses]

The poor man. The poor, ridiculous, *useless* man. Before that I always thought he would be my rock. Some rock. As soon as I got something terrible, as soon as I really needed him, he cracked.

Oh, Gary.

I think it was hardest on you. Even though I was the one who was sick. I think you sent Charlie away because you saw your father go away and you thought it was the right thing to do.

[pauses]

He came back. A year later. Once I was clean. Where he was that year, I don't know, exactly. He sent most of his paycheck to us. That was something. I had friends help me out. But he was gone. I learned about his weaknesses, then. More than I had ever wanted to learn about any-one. Some people don't have the capacity to stand up to adversity. They don't have the guts. They withdraw from it. Like animals, really. When they get wounded they hide from the world. It's how they survive. Your father was wounded.

It sounds strange to say. I was the one with the life-threatening cancer, but he was the one who felt wounded. His wife was defective. How horrible for him! And so he slunk into the woods like a dog with a broken leg.

[pauses]

Is this hard for you? To learn the true nature of your father? It should be. It was hard for me.

But you see how you thought Charlie should do the same thing? You were emulating your father. Charlie never came back. Partly because you didn't want him to, but mostly because you outgrew him.

Which was fine. We all outgrow our childhoods. Or we should.

I think I outgrew your father too. I had a whole year to think about it. I knew when I got better he would return. I knew that in my bones, the way a woman *knows* she's pregnant even before a test shows it.

And I was right. He came trundling back with his tail between his legs. He said he was sorry, he said he had no excuse and he didn't expect me to forgive him, but he hoped I would take him back.

Well.

I had a decision to make. For a year I wanted to hurt him. Such a terrible admission. To you and to myself. But it was true. I would have been happy to read about his death in the newspaper. I would have hoped for a particularly gruesome and painful death. And I would have reveled in the details.

But here's the thing about love, Gary.

It's a physical process.

When he came back he didn't walk into the house. He knocked on the door. Even though he still had a key. Even though it was still his house and his family still lived in it. He knocked. Quietly.

When I answered the door and saw him, I wanted to hate him.

But I couldn't.

There was something about him standing there. How he *looked* like he was sorry. His whole body crumpled in on itself. Me, who had just been through the cancer treatments, I was still thin and weak, I was still trying to get back on my solid feet, on solid ground, I could see it. I could see by the way he stood and looked at me and the way his eyes and face hung, the way his own agony, his own self-loathing must have hurt him. I could see a kindred soul, someone knocked back by life, like I was.

I forgave him. On the spot.

I took him back. It might have been the wrong thing to do. I don't know. You were glad to have him in the house again. I think. By that time you and I had become our own unit. We were doing fine. You could have gone on forever without him, I think, but I suppose it was fine that you didn't. It was good you had your father around.

The second time I got cancer, all those years later, the round that killed me, that time he stayed.

I sometimes wondered if he stayed out of guilt from the first time.

I understood wanting to be alone with my misery then. Sometimes I wanted him to leave. I would tell him to leave. But I suppose he learned something. The second time he stayed with me to the end.

Grumbling the whole time, but he stayed.

[pauses]

Not that this story has a happy ending. We're not in some blissful afterlife together, on a cloudy porch in our rocking chairs. It doesn't work that way.

I don't know where your father is.

But a funny thing.

I found Charlie.

Can you believe it? He was roaming around and saw me before I saw him. He came to me. I didn't recognize him at first, then he told me who he was. He was Charlie. Gary's friend.

I saw what you liked about a giant rabbit. I saw how you could love something you made up.

I took to him like he was my own son.

So funny to say. So strange to think.

But it's true.

He still roams around. He still goes off by himself. He's an animal, you know. That's what they do. But he comes back to me and we have a nice time together.

When Charlie's here with me, it all seems bearable, the whole crazy business of life.

And death.

god

. . . the next the next the next the next the next and now we come to gary hawken who lies unmoving except for certain internal organs and squishy processes unseen by those who attend him and love him and even some who do not care for him which is as it should be since no one can be loved by everyone and any person who says different is ignorant or demented or both and i have in mind even those that invoke me for their views of the universe and morality and how everything fits together since they constantly speak for me when i need no one to speak for me and never have needed anyone to speak for me not since the beginning of time since i was there when the word first made itself known and i have done without punctuation or capitalization or even paragraphing which is all the work of those who came after me who tried to tame the word and the unruly unkempt wildness of the word which cannot be tamed can only be diluted by such contrivances that act to weaken the power of the words when in reality all that anyone needs is conjunctions to link the endless instances of the word in a nonstop concatenation of meaning as the words the words the words they all pile up they all come crashing into your brain but the only word that matters is the first word om and now repeat it three times and you will see how it lives in your heart in your brain your tired brain om om om and such meaning there the birth the cry the love the mystery all contained in the one word but one word is not enough oh no one word only begins the journey and so more words come more words arrive and crash on the shore of your brain on the edge of consciousness all the words all the words all the words in a stream but you do not want this you want some control some domestic version of the wild word and this does not surprise me since you are a nesting people and please be clear that i did not create you though you wish it to be so you have always wanted it so that you might live with no responsibility for yourselves you have always wanted to be made from something else from some other substance or some other realm even though you must know you must realize in your heart of hearts that you are not something else you are just instances of the material world and your heart itself will die and your flesh will decay and you will falter and stumble and trip and struggle and yes even you gary hawken who does not move who does not move you will live and die just as everything else in the material world will live and die and this is not a dismal prospect even though you find it so and even though you will wail and cry against it shedding tears endlessly like words flowing like water coming down from mountains like starlight streaming through space like me flowing everywhere everywhere everywhere until even i must pause at the abundance even i who cannot abide the tics you put on my words yes even i conclude that there is too much isness in existence and i grant you the time needed to take it all in and understand it as best you can which is not all that good and i am sure you understand that at least some of you especially the game players among you always looking for rules always taking the elements and concocting laws to make them slide up against each other in a way that makes sense to you like stories make sense thinking laws are stories thinking rules are stories thinking all the ways that things interact are nothing but stories and this i must say is a shrewd observation that some of you have made for in the beginning you realize there was no story and not until the first word the first sound the first bellow came did a story emerge a story that has been distorted over the eons but which is still there even for one such as gary hawken who has a name and a history and therefore an ego which at this time is all that is keeping you alive gary hawken all that is bringing some meaning to your existence is words since you do not move and you do not touch the world so the word is all you have these words that come from the people who want you ambulatory and whole and who want you back with them so why not push me away gary why not tell me you are tired of me and my endless prattle bothering you with my coherence my special way of making the world something it is not something it cannot be and do not think that i do not understand your predicament since i was in your position at one time eons ago i was floating in the void with no material existence and no extension of any kind no isness to me but i could not tolerate this i could not allow myself to float through the history of the universe in such a state and i manifested myself yes i did i did i did a kind of bootstrap raising of my own being until i was something more than i was previously which was a revelation to me and to existence if i may be so bold as to speak for existence be- cause because because i discovered much to my surprise and delight that as i manifested myself so too did the universe manifest around me and now gary hawken i offer you this revelation completely without ties

or obligations to me in any way and i mean that most sincerely so pay
heed and listen carefully when i tell you that you too can manifest the
world and all the solid glory of the world and all the life of the world
exactly as i did exactly as i still do and as all sentient beings do since let
me tell you something else something you might call a secret but which
is no secret at all but the very obvious principle of the universe and all
that it contains and that principle very simply stated is that life comes
from will and nothing more and i do realize that many even including
you gary hawken will find this statement a mystery and a conundrum
and an enigma but that is your brain getting in the way because will has
nothing to do with brain and you must find a way to let that part of you
allow the sliding of will to flow into you and then you will wake wake
wake up and you will find that all this was as a dream had all the substance of a dream can you do that gary hawken can you find the faith
to believe in yourself can you can you can you and i am asking you
incessantly to prod you into realizing the truth which is that you can of
course you can because i was nothing once and i was only potential once
and i rose up and even though you have made of me something i am
not it is no great matter as i am all things and will be all things and all
things come from me but i am not unique in this gary hawken and i
want you to know that you have just as much potential as i do and can
manifest life at least as much as i can and i feel you know gary hawken
i feel you drifting away and my powers are not as i had hoped i had
wished to be able to drop in on you to find you as you are and move you
to what you might be but gary hawken you fight me you do you do you
do but i do not see why such a one as yourself would choose such a
course of action and so i now ask you directly gary hawken i ask you
what is it that is so comforting about where you are what is it that com-
pels you to reject the tumbling joy of interacting with the world and i

ask you with all due respect and knowing that perhaps you do have a
good reason for your epic withdrawal your brooding need for alone
time raised to the nth power but you must see that such is not productive to you or to those around you for they are filled with grief and
sorrow and rage and only you can assuage that energy that negative
spark that robs all those around you of their will for i believe i know
what you are battling gary hawken yes i do i see it in you because i have
seen it in myself i often have the urge to withdraw just as you have done
and i pull back pull back pull back until i see what i am doing and then
i tell myself to stop to step forward again to understand that my powers
are limited but they are still my powers and even though everything i
see around me everything you think that i have created will die die die
it is not a reason to withdraw from life so you see gary hawken you must
embrace the reality of demise can you do that can you be brave enough
to step forward and see that the end will come but that the end does not
define the now can you take that leap of faith as i have done in the past
and do even now and continue to do as an example to you and people
like you gary hawken people like you who do not know what god is and
cannot fathom that god may be something that none of you have conceived of yet so you say god is a white robed old man or god is a snake
or god is a feeling or god is the oneness or god is the maker or god is
something else something else you have dreamed up but god is not a
dream god is me and i am none of those things but i am all of those
things because i do not exist except as you conceive of me and even
though your conception may be flawed it only means that i am flawed
but that is not sufficient reason to remain aloof and withdrawn so will
you take that lesson now gary hawken and will you rise will you rise
will you rise up now and see the world for what it is which is a reflection
of you because nothing you perceive has a reality beyond yourself and

just what do you think i am gary hawken this voice you hear where do you think it comes from do you think it has coalesced out of the ether and descended upon you is that what you think gary hawken because if it is you are mistaken since the voice is you and only you all these voices are just you talking to yourself and is that what you want is that how you want your life to be to continue to exist because if that is what you truly want then you can have that you can continue in this way for an eternity if that will make you happy but i do not think such a thing will make you or anyone happy and i wish i had the power to look inside you and see what you intend see what your mind wants but it is closed to me as all minds are since my powers are limited you see and i cannot tell if i am wasting my effort here in trying to rouse you or if my efforts are proving to have some effect but you know gary hawken it is all the same in the end for me and i do not wish to make you feel insignificant because though you are insignificant you are also significant and that is the enduring paradox of life and of love that we are nothing but we are something and you should embrace that dichotomy you should find solace in the simultaneous existence of those opposing views and when you do that gary hawken when you embrace that truth and live in the eternal present with those opposing truths simmering in your brain you will find the reason for living and that is all you need gary hawken all anyone needs is to understand and embrace the opposites that are all around us and coddle us and prod us and point us to something other than ourselves because even though we are alone we are also accompa-nied by others and though we die we also live and though we weep we also laugh and though we wither we also prosper and though we fly we also crawl and though we hate we also love and all of these at the same time because we are not ordinary beings though we are made of ordi-nary things and you must see that gary hawken you must see how your conception of me and of what god is and is not must by necessity be a complex thing and a simple thing can you see that gary hawken can you see the reflection of me in you can you see that you are mundane and exalted all at the same time can you see how the universe ignores you and implores you can you hear the om calling you the meaningless om om om that is full of meaning and nonsense and wisdom and gibberish and it is a call to action and forgiveness for inaction and a sign of indifference and a clue to love love love that permeates everything and yet is a delicate bit of insignificance that rolls around the arena of existence like a tiny marble or a minuscule mote of dust and so you might wonder gary hawken why i am devoting my energies to your case as it were to your situation that has more to it than you can imagine that has more to it in the fuller measure of the world than you can understand for you are like a tree weeping sap and i am an insect drawn to your pain and falling into the sap and i am trapped there by your unwillingness to see by your inability to step out of the tissue of your own closing down your own tightly wrapped and closely guarded self but you cannot see what i see which is that you are not a monologue you are not the sum of these voices and yet you are the sum of them and that is the paradox that is what i am trying to tell you is that you are a concatenation of the voices do you see that do you see that you contain multitudes do you see how you will always be a conglomeration of things and yet you will be your own pure self and do you also see that the most important word after om which was the first word is the word and because and always builds it builds and builds and builds forever if necessary and will find a way to add things to other things so if you find yourself alone just think of the word and think of how all those ands linked together form a life they form a story a tale an infinity of tales and pull them into you gary hawken please pull them all to you because i am eternal but i am

finite and i cannot spend all my days and years here with you trying to
nurse you back to something that the universe recognizes when it is
evident to me that my nursing and my prodding can do very little for
you at this point because even though i am the supreme being as you
have conceived me it is also evident that i am nothing to you i am nothing to anyone and so the essential paradox is fulfilled exactly as i have
been telling you and you can see it now you must see it as i see it for we
are all the same you and i and the gary hawken that i know is completely misrepresented and you see how i come back to that observation
like a criminal returning to the scene of his crime you see how i will
return to this theme this nick in my skin this catch in my throat this
skip in my heartbeats this nagging thought in my brain that is you always you clamoring for my attention in your passive way that will not
abide my words but cannot dispel yourself of my words and so i want
you to consider what i am to you gary hawken what my name means to
you my name that is god that is a murky thing in your brain but also a
sharp image in your brain and a distant concept but a personal impres-
sion but do not think on it too long because thinking is the eternal pause
and you can think yourself to death and did you know that gary hawken
that you can make yourself ruminate and cogitate and ponder and
contemplate until the stars burn out and the galaxies deflate and the
atoms decay and there's nothing left of existence but your silly silly
silly thoughts pinging here and clanking there and trying to give yourself some kind of purpose in life by being a thinker a voice enhancer
and a voice manipulator and a voice synthesizer but you know there are
machines to do that sort of thing now and we don't need you to do it
anymore if we ever did which i don't think we did not really gary
hawken not really because you know what the universe hears when you
think and you send out your thoughts and you broadcast all the voices

you have inside you and you think they are from outside do you know what the universe hears when they look at the mirror that is you do you conceive of what they hear gary hawken what they hear is you going om om om and they laugh gary hawken they laugh because it is a meaningless word a meaningless syllable but it is also everything there is and nothing there is and i am done with you now gary hawken i am done with this monologue this voice that you wish to have in you this voice that you find somewhere and draw to yourself gary hawken there are so many voices and they all say the same thing because there is nothing else to say because the universe is you gary hawken and the voice is you gary hawken and god is you gary hawken and you have no reason to doubt this because you have the power and do not need anyone or anything else and never have needed and never will need and so i take this voice this godlike thing in your ear tunneling and whispering and hoping for something and i go on to the next station to the next hope that needs kindling to the next one that beckons to the next one that asks a question of me and makes me think the first punctuation mark had to be a question mark because it is the way to bring the next into the conversation it is the way to draw the next the next the next the next the next . . .

mother nature

First he comes around to chat so now it's my turn. Is that it? Is that the way you've set this up?

You are quite the manipulator, aren't you? Stretched out like some inert piece of—well, nothing. Nothing is inert. Everything is alive. Even you, with your wild imagination calling up all of us icons to come talk to you. We're like cable television for you, aren't we? Satellite TV.

Here's my question for you, though:

What have you got against life?

[pauses]

No answer? It's a simple question. You've got the power to step into life, so why aren't you exercising that power?

[pauses]

Some of the voices before mine have remarked how you make them want to speak to you. Your silence induces them into spilling secrets about themselves. I have to tell you, your spell isn't working on me. I have nothing to say to you.

[pauses]

I know Death came by here. He comes by here a lot. You are like his nexus of—something. I'm not sure what, exactly.

[pauses]

Here's what I see.

And please correct me if I get any of this wrong.

You got into an accident. You bumped your head. Now you're pouting and you want someone to take care of your boo-boo.

That about covers it, doesn't it? Being a big baby suited you for some reason, so you decided to become a big baby.

You like that people are disrupting their lives for you. You adore all this attention.

And what's more, you'd be more than happy to continue like this for a long time. Maybe for eternity. Being a grown-up is too much work. Too much responsibility. You never wanted children. You never wanted a job and bills.

[pauses]

Am I close to the truth? I'll bet I am. I think I've probably nailed it right on the head.

[pauses]

My man, Death, he was the same way, you know. It surprised the hell out of me. I thought we had something important, something that would last. I thought he was like me, willing to better himself if he had the chance. Willing to look at himself with a critical eye. An appraising eye. An eye that could see past his eternal life and catch a glimpse of something more. Something bigger than himself. Because he had a lot of power. He probably told you I liked his robes. The mystery. I'll have to admit there was something about the way he looked that caught my attention. So confident. Very appealing. But there was more. He had an amazing talent for relieving suffering. I saw it and I was amazed by it. I wasn't quite so in love with the *method* he chose to relieve that suffering. I thought he would outgrow that in time, especially under my influence.

It didn't happen.

And I was okay with that. You probably think I'm making that up, but I'm not. Not at all. I struggled with it for a while, tried to see how what he did had some redeeming qualities to it, and I finally decided that he was correct. He'd been doing this for eternity, after all. And life had its flaws. It was not a perfect thing, so his yin of death to my yang of life, it was a good fit.

I remember telling him, fairly early on in the relationship, but far enough along that we were more than new boyfriend and girlfriend, that I respected his work and hoped he was able to continue it for as long as he wanted.

And he reciprocated. He said without what I did, there would be no reason for him to go on.

Very flattering, I can tell you, when a man, the man you love, tells you he can't go on without you. Scary, in its way, but flattering.

So I just wanted to make that clear. In case he didn't tell you that. He thinks I'm some kind of manipulative woman trying to control him, but that isn't the case at all. I didn't want to control anything.

But then our child was born.

You're a father. You know what that does to your life. To your world. Everything changes.

I wanted things to be the same for Death. I respected him and knew he was settled in his ways, but the child. The child.

I could not have him floating around the house in those robes and carrying that scythe. It was not right. It was scary, and children don't need that kind of scare in their lives.

So I merely *suggested* that he might, now that we had a child, he might *consider* doing something with his life that was a little more conducive to allowing our child a life which did not include being scared to death every time she/he saw his/her father. A reasonable request. Not a demand. Not an ultimatum. Simply a request that he see the reality of our new situation.

[pauses]

There comes a time in a relationship when you see the other person for what they are. Not for what you hoped they would be, or for what they represented themselves as at the beginning. Or for what *they* hope they are. That time for me came when I saw him struggling with the new reality of our life.

Oh, he tried. I'll give him that. He put down his scythe. Pulled the hood off his head, and began to wear flowers. It thrilled my heart to see him try as hard as he did. I thought then that I had made exactly the right choice becoming intimate with him.

[pauses]

But here's the sad part.

He was not made for life. His constitution did not allow him to go on for long without taking life.

Can you understand how devastating that was for me? I had hooked up with Death, and nothing he or I could do would ever make him give up on death. Not for real. Not for long term.

I looked into his face, looked into the face of Death, and I knew. He looked haggard. All the joy had drained out of him. His eyes drooped, his cheeks were hollow, and he didn't shave. He had stubble, where before he would never let himself go. He shuffled around in slippers and his robes, well, they began to look a little bedraggled, like an old and ratty housecoat.

It was repellent, such sadness. Such pitiable sadness.

I do believe he frightened the child even more in that state than when he was in his power as death. Or Death, to be more precise. Because if anyone was their job, that was my old man. His name was his description. His name was his entire being.

I didn't have the heart to let him go on in such a woefully diminished manner, so I suggested that he might want to think about returning to his former glory. The life he had abandoned. For his family. I emphasized that what he had attempted was noble and I appreciated it no end, but I could not see him suffer as he was suffering.

And do you know what he did?

To this day I think of it and I shed a tear.

He said no.

He said I was right. That he needed to think of our child and how he was affecting him/her. He was going through a rough transition, but once he got his mind right, he was going to embrace this new way of being. He'd figure out something that would help all the creatures living with pain and debilitating conditions. He would find a way to ease the boredom for people living forever. He just needed some time and if he got some to devote to his new mode, he would be hunkey-dorey.

Oh, I so wanted him to be that man. I so wanted to soften Death and make him more like me. I admit it. I wanted him to do as he offered.

But I saw the consequences. The way life proliferated unchecked. Because I wasn't changing. I was still creating life. I was granting the bounty of fertility left and right. I was doing my calling with no letup.

Trees were growing, creatures were multiplying, the whole grand entanglement of life was proceeding with fullness and bounty.

I was fulfilling my destiny.

So I told my old man, I told Death, that I had been wrong to tell him he was wrong. I implored him to practice his craft once more.

I told him to take the things that I had made, the things that I had given life to, and I told him to kill them. Not indiscriminately, of course. But when their time came, when their destiny had been fulfilled, I told him to do what he did best.

I felt like I was encouraging a mass murderer.

I know it's not like that. I know we all have a place in the process and if nothing dies then all the resources will get used up and soon there will be nothing left for anyone, I get that. I'm not without some mental faculties. But it was still hard.

I saw his hesitation.

But I saw that if he continued on his course then *he* was going to die. And I was Mother Nature. I could not be the agency of his death.

Oh, my head was spinning with all the ramifications of what we were doing. What we were attempting, which was nothing less than a re-ordering of the cosmos.

That isn't what we intended when we got together. Certainly not what we intended when we made the child. But that is what we were stuck with, where we had come to.

Our tenderest moment together happened then, while I searched his eyes for some sense of what we had done and what he would have to go back to doing.

He saw where we were headed. Fully comprehended the ramifications of going back. We both did, I think. We had this unspoken thing in that moment. This spark that we carried together.

I wanted that moment to go on forever, but it could not. I like to imagine that he wanted that too. I don't know. I've never asked him. It's still too tender. Maybe, in a few million years, I will. Find a moment when we both aren't busy doing what we do, and have a good heart-to-heart with him.

Until then, I asked him if he would do one thing. If he would carry a rose with him. Just for me.

He agreed.

I was so happy. In a melancholy way.

He put the rose on his sleeve. Wore it smartly and the bathrobe aspect of his costume evaporated. He shaved. His face brightened, and his cheeks filled out. He was back.

[pauses]

And I loathed him.

I'm not sure I can convey to you the extent of my disgust. It was centered on him, for the work he did. But it also extended to me. Because I had agreed that he needed to go back to killing. I saw the wisdom of it. The necessity of it.

And yet.

There was something in me, in my basic makeup, that found it abhorrent in the extreme.

We are all complex beings. Every one of us. We do not necessarily behave in rational ways. I certainly do not.

I tried to hide my feelings from him, but even Death has some acquaintance with empathy, and he saw what was happening. He took to staying out later than necessary, just to avoid my contempt.

Oh, it was the worst time of my life. Knowing that the father of my child, the father of what would most likely be my *only* child, was a repellent creature to me.

[pauses]

What more is there to say? We limped along like that for a while. Finally, both of us seeing that we could not go on like this, could not allow our child to constantly see us in such an adversarial setting, he quietly moved out.

I do believe my child missed him. But only for a while.

I confess that I loved the house much more without his heavy presence, filling the rooms with despair and melancholy.

Of course, now we have found a new life, in which we do respect each other, and we share time with our child. It is better this way.

[pauses]

Oh, I guess everyone is right. You do invite storytelling. Somehow you are the tabula rasa that needs filling with tales and anecdotes.

Myths. Adventures. Farces. Parables.

You are so hungry for them. What is that about? You don't want to live, but you want to hear about other people's lives?

Tell me what's troubling you. Tell me why you want to continue sleeping.

[pauses]

Don't you want to see your children? Don't you want to see them grow up?

Don't you want to see your wife?

I remember when I blessed you with children. Yes, that was my doing. I'm Mother Nature. I give life. I brought that spark to fruition for you and Melody. I did it twice. You were so happy. Do you remember that? Do you remember the happiness I brought you?

[pauses]

I don't know why I'm bothering here. I really don't. You are so stubborn.

And this third one. Not born yet, but that was me, too. I made that happen. With a little help from you and Melody, granted, but still.

Look how I've brought all these birds, flying around your head. Do you hear them? They're so happy. All they want to do is fly and sing. Do you hear the air rushing over their feathers? Such a soothing sound. It makes me want to live, just hearing that sound, the way the wind calls up the sound of the wings. That's life, right there. That's what I can't do without. I wish it was something you decided you couldn't do without.

There's one on your nose.

[laughs]

Do you feel that? It's browsing around your nose, looking for grubs and things. Seeds. It's not going to find any. You don't have any.

Yet.

[laughs]

Surely you feel that. The little thing is barely half a pound. Maybe less. It's a trifle. If you caught it in your hand you could crush it. My dear ex, he could wink at it and it would keel over in an instant. But it has life. Even as small and insignificant as it is, it harbors the spark and does not question that the spark is real and true and right.

It's got this bird brain that wouldn't fill half a thimble, and it knows. It knows in every cell of its being, in every groove of every feather, that life is for living. So why is it so difficult for you?

There's another one. Scratching around your cheek.

They make me laugh, they do.

[pauses]

I created them, so maybe I'm biased, but there is no greater delight that watching creatures. Watching any living thing. Even plants. You need to watch plants. They move. Slowly, but they move. Maybe you think you're like a plant, but you're not. You're not partaking of the essence of your being, not like a plant does. A plant interacts with its environment. You aren't doing that. You're just lying there, hoping other people will live your life for you. Do you see the absurdity of what you are doing? Do you see that you are violating your very essence?

I'll bet Death, when he talked to you, he said you needed to decide. Did he?

With his rose-adorned sleeve fluttering in the breeze, I bet. Maybe brandishing his scythe, holding it high and waving it like a lightning bolt. Did he? I can see him doing that. I can see him looking down on you. Decide decide decide. Why is it so difficult? Make up your mind. Is it life or is it death? Stop existing in this limbo.

[pauses]

I admit I don't know what he did. I've never watched him practice his craft. He says he relieves suffering and I believe him. But I can't watch. I can't. I think if I ever did, it would so violate my own sense of what's right that I might be struck blind. So I don't watch. I haven't watched. Was I close? Is that the way it was?

I like to think so. I like to think that he is dramatic. Nothing wrong with drama. It's another way of embracing life, and my old man, despite his name and his profession, despite what he does, he's full of life.

Can you grasp the paradox? Everything is full of both, you know. My own child is born of life and death. That taught me things. Made me see the world anew, even at my age. And now it's your turn.

I'm not going to brandish anything over you. I'm not going to call down the powers and make you decide.

But you really need to.

The time is drawing close.

You've been here, for, what? Months now. Getting close to a year. Everyone is getting weary of this.

[pauses]

Melody has taken to gardening. Do you understand why? Do you comprehend the magnitude of this?

I understand. Because that's what I do. That's my calling. I plant seeds, and then I water them and make sure they get sun, and then I watch life grow.

Not literally, but metaphorically. That's what I do.

Shoo shoo shoo.

I just brushed away the birds. Did you feel them fly away? Their wing tips brushed your eyebrows.

Your wife, your old lady, the mother of your children, she wants you to live so much that she has started to grow a garden. It's like she has done all she can to bring you back and she feels like she has failed, so now she has moved her energy and her sorrow to her garden. Can you conceive of how important that garden is for her?

Gary Hawken, *you* are more important than that garden. More important than anything, and you need to acknowledge that.

[pauses]

But I'm not the first to tell you what needs to happen here. I'm not the first one to make clear your options.

I'm aware that in some ways I am asking you to do a little thing. The tiniest thing. You're balanced on the slimmest edge, teetering first this way, to life, and then that way, to death. And I'm aware that it is an infinitesimal nudge one way or another that will decide your fate. I see that. So I'm asking, with all due respect and with all due compassion for your situation, I'm asking you to make the supreme effort of will that will move that infinitesimal nudge to my side.

Death can wait.

That's what I have learned in my life and my work. Death is in no hurry.

I lived with the guy. He moved like a slug. When he moved at all.

Here.

I'm leaving you a rose. In your hand. Don't feel like you need to grasp it. Just let it lie there. It'll tell you what you need to know. It'll wait for you, too.

It knows you'll make the right decision.

mario milosevic

And what of me? Have I made the right decisions?

I like to think you donated your body to literature, but that's not exactly true. It's much more accurate to say I coerced your body for the sake of my book.

First, the title of the book. It was the working title, the one that came to me as soon as I thought of your story. Then I hesitated. I was concerned that people might think of *The Vagina Monologues* by Eve Ensler, which is a well-known play, performed widely and often. I let my mind cast around for an alternative title, but my wife, the novelist Kim Antieau, thought *The Coma Monologues* to be a fine title, so I decided to put my faith in her good judgement and have kept the working title as the actual title.

I have seen a performance of *The Vagina Monologues* by the way. I remember it as funny and energizing.

I was going to give my book a subtitle: *A Philosophical Inquiry*, because in many ways that's how I think of it, but decided against it. Not very commercial, and I do want people to *want* to read this book.

Did I create you?

Yes. Before I had the idea of you, only a couple of months ago, you were nothing. Less than nothing. You were not even an idea.

Did I create you?

No. You have no existence. You are merely an idea. I have tried to make you as believable as possible, by giving you the accoutrements of a life, but in the end, you are nothing. You have no physical existence. I cannot be credited with creation if the result of that creation does not exist.

Did I create you?

Maybe. It could also be that you came to me from some mysterious place no one understands. Creativity is a mystifying process and perhaps what happened is that you already existed in some Platonic ideal realm and all I did was write you down. I acted as a stenographer to the muses.

All three are viable possibilities, and I could spend the balance of my monologue going over each of them in excruciating detail, but that would not serve me or you, so I will use, as a working theory, the thought that in fact I did create you. It makes things simpler and boosts my ego.

I have this strong perception and memory that I did think of you. One afternoon you came to me: a man in a coma, listening to the voices of his life. It was an arresting image: delicate, in its way, even precarious, but filled with possibilities. Who owned the voices? Were they real? Imaginary? Why were there voices? Were you going to die? How close to death were you and was there some urgency to keep you from death? Were the voices for your amusement only, or did they add up to something else, something more powerful? All those questions rose up in the minutes after thinking of you. I knew I had something that needed writing because you didn't go away the next day. You were still in my mind.

But even after I thought of you, a person in a coma, you weren't much. You had no name when I began. About a third of the way through the writing your last name emerged. Or a variant of it. Because at first I wanted to call you Hawke to evoke the idea of a bird. I wanted people to think of you as a flying creature, as someone who *could* wake from your slumber and take to the air, at least metaphorically. I added the terminal N a few days later. I wanted to blunt the metaphor slightly, to try to simply give a hint of an avian aspect. Your first name did not come to me until a few days after that. Gary. An ordinary name for an ordinary person. Gary Hawken, a normal everyday guy with the potential to rise to the air and soar.

Yes, actually, I really did think of all those things. I tried to work through the reaction that the sound of your name might evoke in someone, specifically, the mythical reader that might stumble upon this book.

The accident that put you in your present condition, on the other hand, did not occupy a lot of my thoughts. I just needed something to put you into a coma, some expedient and believable method.

Did you know that many coma patients get that way from car accidents? Very common. So I gave you a car accident. Made sure it was the sort of thing that would bump your head but otherwise leave you more or less intact, and *boom!* here you are.

I gave you a family. After all, an ordinary man usually has a family. I had Melody's name long before I had yours. In fact, I had her name in my mind before I wrote the first line of the book. I knew someone named Melody about twenty-five years ago. Your wife is nothing like her at all. She just shares the name. I wanted to give the idea of optimism and a musically suggestive name fit the bill for me. Melody is nothing if not optimistic. She is the engine of the story, the power that moves the plot forward, the will that makes everything happen.

The Melody I used to know was not like the Melody in this book. She was a newspaper editor. Think of a chain-smoking, hard-drinking cynic. But with a heart of gold. She wanted to see the right thing done, but seldom did and had to report on the dire consequences of bad decisions, bad luck, inept officials, and corrupt people from all walks of life. I think it hurt her, this parade of misery. I don't blame her for her diminished idealism. It was probably necessary for her own protection. If you write about the failures of people for long enough, it would be tough not to catch at least a touch of cynicism.

But my Melody doesn't have that. My Melody, the one I invented and the one I gave you, *your* Melody, always thinks you'll wake up. Every day she goes to the hospital and she *believes*. That's how she gets through the day. The days. She assumes you will come back to her. She's just as real or as unreal as you are. You came from the same place, wherever that is. I might just as well be addressing her in this monologue.

Just to get a few things out of the way:

I don't believe in God. Or any gods. I don't disrespect anyone who does, but I don't automatically accord their beliefs respect either. Mostly I leave that aspect of people's lives alone. There's a reason for that old saying about never discussing politics and religion.

In politics I'm left-leaning. An aging socialist with some doubts about certain aspects of socialism. I like the idea of universal health care and employing the power of the state to help people have better lives, but I also see the value of personal property, especially the individual ownership of land. It may well be the single most important element of a free society: for without personal ownership, then you are always at the whim of someone else. And yet. The accumulation of wealth and land, when concentrated in one person, confers the power of coercion on that person. So it's a balancing act, trying to find the sweet spot where freedom truly flourishes. I don't expect anyone to respect my beliefs in the political sphere. We get many of them from random events in our lives which create pockets of biased and myopic realities in our minds, not a nuanced and astute analysis of the truth.

Many readers parse books looking for biographical aspects of the author's life. It is the second most common question writers of fiction get: *How much of this book is about you?* (The most common is: *Where do you get your ideas?*) If you could read this book, you who are the central character of the book, I wonder, would you ask the same question? Would you want to know how much of you comes from me?

Maybe. When I write a book, I like to think that if I were to meet the character I created, he or she would have enough life to be curious about his or her origin. I haven't investigated the situation, but I'm sure there are critics who believe any work of fiction is only the distilled essence of the writer's biography. I wonder, do you believe that? I wonder, if you had the power of animation, would you be content with thinking that you are only the light of me, streaming through the prism of this disjointed narrative? But maybe you don't know enough about me to tell. Perhaps, since I know everything about you, you should know something about me.

Very well. For comparison's sake, and for the benefit of both you and the reader, I'll give point-by-point comparisons about certain aspects of our lives.

You grew up in Sudbury, Ontario. So did I.

You had no sisters or brothers. I had one of each.

You had a friend who shared your interest in science fiction. So did I.

You graduated from the University of Waterloo. So did I.

You studied engineering. I was a math and philosophy grad.

You moved to Toronto after graduation. I moved to Michigan.

You got married. So did I.

You had children. I do not.

You own a house. My wife and I rent.

You're in a coma. I'm not.

I think that covers the highlights. There are some congruences, but I think it's safe to say that we are not the same people. You are not a mirror of me. I am not the model for you.

Or maybe you are.

For example, my favorite writer when I was growing up was Isaac Asimov. I never called him on the phone, as I had you do, but I knew about his life. I knew where he lived and that he had children and was divorced and remarried and I knew how many books he wrote. I really liked *The Gods Themselves*. I haven't read it since it first came out, and I am somewhat cautious about doing so, since reading a book one loved as a kid can be very disappointing.

So, surely, some aspects of you are also aspects of myself.

Except I don't want to be in a coma. Who would?

Maybe that's the crux of the book, the question that all the monologues skate around but never quite confront. Who would be happy to live asleep for months and years on end?

At first, it seems a ridiculous question. No one could actually be *happy* in that condition. Could they?

But consider:

Some people happily withdraw from the world. Certain monks find enlightenment in solitude. Certain people, frightened of human contact, find solace in their own company. Many people crave the experience, common in literature and movies, of being lost, of completely falling into the story so that their own lives disappear and they are swept along on the current of story.

So it was not too much of a stretch for me to believe that someone—you, for example—might find happiness and contentment in removing yourself from the world. At least for a time.

And yet.

I could not let you alone. I could not create you as a withdrawn human and leave it at that. You had to have something going on with you for me to care, and for any hope that readers would care. So I gave you voices.

Your being, your entire life, became a collection of voices.

How does that sit with you? Are you satisfied with the fate I gave you?

You do not answer.

Ah, well. That is how I made you after all, so I cannot criticize you for behaving according to the parameters I set. But I want you to have an independent life. I want to be able to question you and I want you to question me.

The futile wish of a creator, I suppose. What I want from my flights of imagination is some kind of verisimilitude. An illusion, surely, but life itself must be considered some species of illusion, don't you think? We have no conception of reality. We make what we call reality out of the perceptions of our minds. I do it. Everyone I know does it. We wander around in the soup of existence and taste this morsel here, that bit of spiciness there, and we make of all those tastes and sensations a world. But it is a personal world, nothing that can reliably translate into certainty.

Forgive me. I was a philosophy major, after all. We spent our time questioning reality, and questioning the theories and writings of those who came before us and questioned reality in their way. I think all that questioning was supposed to help us come to some understanding of how the world worked.

You'll notice that in the monologue by your former professor, she explicitly states that questions do not bring any kind of enlightenment.

Which roughly corresponds to my own beliefs. Questions can obscure the truth, but they will never reveal the truth. They can lead you to the truth, if deployed judiciously, but too often we don't know what questions to ask and therefore we end up more confused than before we asked the questions.

I suppose that's why zealots are so happy in their zealotry. They have gone beyond questioning and are content with their current beliefs.

For myself, I think that beliefs are mostly arbitrary. It's a belief I picked up during some random reading I did when I was about fourteen years old.

That was when I was reading fantastic literature by the bushel. During one long stretch of close to a year, I was reading a book a day. Mostly science fiction novels and short story collections. I loved the short stories. Chock full of ideas and incident, and they were over in a few pages and I could plunge into another story, with a whole new set of ideas and incidents. It was a glorious waste of my time, but I would not have had it any other way.

I was not completely non-physical. I ran track at school. The hundred yard dash was my event. I also played hockey, baseball, and soccer, as weather permitted for each sport. These were all neighborhood pickup games. I tried out for organized hockey once, but everyone was so intense and intent on winning that no one had any *fun* playing the game, least of all me, so I quit.

I did not give you much of a physical life. It wasn't my fault. You're in a coma, remember? You don't have much going on in your life of a physical nature.

From the beginning, I was determined that you would hear voices that didn't exist. The mythical creatures, the animals, the dead people, the made up, the quirky creations of the human mind.

I want to know what you think of those. I want to know your opinion of things. Is that irrational of me?

I want people to wonder: are the voices real, or are they simply the random firings of your mind? Surely a centaur does not speak to you. But perhaps he does. Perhaps he is as real as anyone else. And your wife, Melody, singing your praises, and ringing up the voices from your past, she seems real enough, a manifestation of fierce life, but she may be as illusory and imaginary as the centaur. How is anyone to know, for sure? How am I to know? I could orchestrate things to make them more clear, but a certain tension would then drain away from the experience. Better to leave it a question.

We are drawing close to the end, and ignorance begins to take on the aspect of an indulgence. It is not good to let the end come with no resolution. Oh, I know there are books and stories that don't tell their endings. I've written some myself. There's a famous one about the tiger and the lady. You don't know, even when you get to the last word of the last paragraph on the last page, what is going to happen because you don't know what the man has chosen. The last event of the story occurs after the end of the story. That story works because of the main character. He's so full of life that you forgive the author for not playing out his premise to the end. I can't do anything like that here. It would feel like a complete cheat.

I need to decide.

And I need to realize that the decision, if I have done my job up to now, is not in my hands. The preceding events of the narrative, of the monologues, should be strong and convincing enough that my hand is obliged to go one way or the other.

Do you conceive of the fact that your fate is dependent on where my fingers land on the keyboard? How does that make you feel? As a character in a narrative, do you wish it were not so? Do you prefer to think that you have some existence beyond me?

It is even up to me to decide if you have those questions. If your mind goes in that direction. It would be a strange aspect to give you, but I have the power to do so.

For example, I could imagine my own self as a character in a narrative. In the same way that I can imagine myself as being in someone's dream. I just did that. I let my mind go down that path and tried to think what would happen when the dreamer woke up. Obviously, I would cease to be. I would wink out of existence in an instant.

The situation is analogous with you.

What if I decided to delete this file? Erase it from my hard drive? What would happen to you? You'd be gone. Oh, I would have some memory of you, but it would be a dim memory. It would not have the texture of life that I tried to give you in these pages.

So.

Here it is.

Here is the challenge I offer you:

Think of yourself as a creation of a person. Me. Now think of me gone.

Dead.

How does that make you feel, the thought that your existence hangs on such a thin thread?

I will forget about you.

I've spent many hours creating you, but I will create other narratives, other fictions, and you will fade from my memory. Ten or twenty years from now I may come across these pages and might even look at them, maybe read a monologue or two, but you will be foreign to me. You will not be as fresh, as alive, as you are now.

How does *that* make you feel?

Pardon me?

I didn't quite hear you.

Can you repeat it please? I will remain as still as possible, quiet as a ghost, tranquil as a pond, silent as falling snow, and sleepy as a coma patient so I can take in every word you want to tell me.

Now go.

michael cunningham

Doctor Ayles, he had this big fight with the judge. I didn't hear it, but I heard about it. Ayles said he was in charge of your care and that meant no judge could simply tell him what would happen to his patient.

The judge, she's the one who gave me the sentence, she said I had to come talk to you. It's supposed to make me see the wrongness of what I did to you.

Doctor Ayles, he said he didn't care about me. His only concern was for you. I get it. That's what you want in your doctor, someone who's completely dedicated to your recovery.

But the judge still wanted this part of my sentence. Privately, I was rooting for your doctor. I didn't want to come down here unless someone made me. And if your doctor could convince the judge to call it off, I was all for it.

Well, they went back and forth like that for some time. For a few months, actually. The doctor, he brought a suit against the judge, which the judge didn't much care for. It made her dig in even more. And the doctor, well, he was like a pit bull, you know. He was not going to give up control of you.

In the end, your wife stepped in and said it would be fine with her if I came and talked to you.

[pauses]

She's even more dedicated to getting you back than your doctor is. She'll try anything. The doctor, he's got some opinions of what your wife is trying, but he's willing to give her the benefit of the doubt. A lot more than he's willing to give the judge.

[pauses]

So here I am. Nervous as all get-out. I'm still on probation. I got convicted of reckless driving. It could have been a lot worse. They were thinking of taking me down on an attempted manslaughter charge, but the prosecutor said he couldn't get a conviction on that. So reckless driving. I'm a reckless driver. I got a suspended sentence. Couple years probation. Ordered to do counselling. My commercial license revoked for five years. May as well be five centuries because I'm not going to go back to driving after five years. Plus this. This monologue. Confession. I don't know what exactly it is. I'm supposed to talk to you. Apologize. See what condition I put you in so the ramifications of my actions can be made clear to me.

[pauses]

It's my fault. I know I said it was. They told me to. I was supposed to say that in the courtroom, to get the lesser charge.

[pauses]

You jumped the light. Did you know that? Maybe you don't remember. I'm not even sure I should be saying this. They're taping it, and they'll listen to it, and what I'm saying contradicts what they told me to say in court, but I guess I really don't care. Not anymore.

[pauses]

Your wife, Melody, she talked to me. She's not mad at me. That was a big surprise. I would be mad at me, if I was in her position. I'd want to kill me. But not her. Amazing.

I was afraid to meet her. And your kids. They all met with me just before I came in here. I don't know what it is with your wife, but she has this idea that we might have some kind of connection, you know. Because we were both there. Both scared out of our wits at the same time. Me because I crashed into you, and I saw it coming and I couldn't do anything about it. You because you saw me coming and couldn't do anything about it, either. She thinks maybe something cosmic put us in the same place at the same time.

Maybe she's right. I don't know. She'll try anything. Any kind of woo woo if that's what works. If that's what it takes.

Did you hear the horn?

I was hauling several tons of freight, so I couldn't stop, not in time. All I could do was sound the horn. Hooooooooonk hooooooooonk hooooooooonk. Three quick shots. To try to get you to look up, to try to get you to go through the intersection faster.

But you didn't do that.

And now here you are.

[pauses]

It's been a year. I did a little reading about comas. They say people in your condition, they're in a perfect position to wake up. Twelve months is not a long time. Twelve months is nothing. A nice nap.

I hope you wake up.

I'm so sorry for what happened to you.

[pauses]

I've never had an accident before. Not like this. I've hauled freight for millions of miles. Been doing it since I was twenty-four and I'm pushing fifty now, so that's a long time. Guys like me, guys on the road most of the time, we talk about how it's inevitable you'll get in an accident. We have this fatalistic view of the universe, you know. The odds are, if you're in it long enough, you're going to jackknife your rig, or you're going to slide off the road, or sideswipe a car or hit a car. Something. The trick is to retire the day before it happens, so it's still in the future.

I went one day too long for you. And for me. You could say I got early retirement. No one's going to hire me now. I guess I don't blame them. I probably wouldn't hire me either. There're lots of drivers out there. Unemployed ones. Companies have their pick, and someone like me, now, I'm not a prime candidate.

Never much thought about what I was going to do after driving. Now I've got to.

I used to be married, but she left me. Said it was too hard on her, me gone all the time. Tried to get me to take up a different line of work, but that wasn't for me. All I knew was driving truck. She wanted me to go to school. Nope. Forget it. What was I going to do? Learn accounting? I told her when I was home, I was home. I gave her all the attention anyone could want, and she saw that, but she said the nights were lonely. And cold.

Wasn't much I could do about that.

We split up ten years ago. She stuck it out for a long time. I guess I'm grateful for that.

The thing is, I was a long-haul driver when we met. She liked that. Thought it was romantic, I guess. I'm not sure. But people change. Not me. I was the same guy when we split as when we met. I was steady. A rock.

Maybe I was too boring. Maybe she needed someone who would shake things up every once in a while.

Old news.

[pauses]

We're still friends. She calls me up a couple of times a year. I call her. We shoot the breeze. She's remarried and got kids. Not her own. She adopted her new husband's, so she's a mom. I like hearing her talk about them. We never had kids. Maybe that was the problem between us. She wanted kids but didn't want to have them if I wasn't going to be around a lot.

So no kids.

Your wife is pregnant. I don't know if you knew that. The baby's actually due any day now. So you're going to be a father again. For the third time. Hope you wake up in time for it.

The prosecutor tried to say that the reason I hit you is that I was distracted. I had on a CD in my rig. I was listening to a book. You ever do that? In your car? A lot of truckers listen to books. We got a lot of lonely time on the road. We talk to each other on the CB, but sometimes that's too much work, so we listen to books.

What do you think I was listening to when I hit you? You'll never guess.

The Arabian Nights. Scheherazade. She tells these stories to keep herself alive. It's quite a book, man. You get a whole picture of society back then, just from listening to all her crazy stories. You wouldn't want to be alive in that society, especially if you were a woman. We got it lucky here in this country, at this time in history.

You know we had Henry VIII. That king in England who killed his wives. He was like a boy scout compared to the king in *The Arabian Nights*. That was one completely crazy king. Like a serial killer. Every night he'd take a new woman and then he'd kill her. *Every night.* Makes you wonder how the population could put up with something like that, but then, they didn't know any better. Plus, they didn't have any power. Anyway, Scheherazade, she volunteers to save the women by being his bride, but she stays alive by telling him stories and not finishing them until the next day.

She goes on like this for years.

So this book is a collection of those stories. There aren't actually a thousand of them, even though the book says there're a thousand and one of them. There're a lot less.

I was listening to one of them.

You know, I don't even know which one it was now. All I remember is the voice of the narrator. It was a woman's voice, coming through my speakers. I should have turned the CD off. I was in the city. I needed to keep my wits about me. On the highway, it's different. It's easier. Not as hairy. You have to pay attention and everything, of course you do, but it's different. For one thing, there aren't so many little cars around. You can relax a little. Not in the city. You need to keep alert because cars don't have an idea about trucks. They don't know that you have to give trucks room. We can't stop on a dime. We're too big.

But I didn't turn it off. The book. I was listening to it. I wanted to know how this one story ended. It was so important, and now I don't even know what it was. Crazy.

So maybe if I had turned it off, you wouldn't be here, because then maybe I'd have noticed you in front of me, and maybe I would have sounded my horn sooner, and maybe you would have heard it, and maybe you wouldn't be here now. Maybe maybe maybe. All those what-ifs don't add up to much.

That's how it goes, right? We want to change things from what they are to what we want them to be. But sometimes you can't do that. You can't change things. Things are what they are.

[pauses]

This is hard. I don't know how much longer I can do this. I want to fill up the silence. You're so quiet. All I hear is the buzzing of the lights and I can't stand it. I have to say something.

[pauses]

Have to fill up the silence with something.

[pauses]

[sobs]

I don't know.

[pauses]

Maybe it *was* all my fault. I don't know. I thought the light was yellow when I entered the intersection. I was sure of it, but you know, maybe I'm trying to convince myself. Maybe the guilt made me see things the way they weren't. Who knows. Memory is a strange game the brain plays with you. It's never the way it really was. Memory is a storyteller, you know. Embellishes and distorts. Slants and flatters. If all you have of an event is your memory of it, then forget it. You have no idea what happened. All you know is what your brain *wanted* to happen.

So maybe I was in the right and you were in the wrong. Maybe you were in the right and I was in the wrong. I don't know. And no judge is going to convince me that I was definitely in the wrong just because she says so and makes me come down here and talk to you.

I didn't want to come.

But I'm here.

[pauses]

I guess you didn't want to come here either. I get it. Shitty situation for you and I'm the one who put you here. Right or wrong, it was me, my rig.

I get it.

I sold the thing. No use to me anymore.

What am I telling you my troubles for? You've got troubles of your own. Big ones.

My rig had some damage on it. A little dented up in the front from where I hit your car. Nothing serious. That's the thing about cars and big rigs. The car is going to lose every time. Yours got totaled. Well, sure. A big rig smashed into it. What else was going to happen to it?

[laughs]

Yeah. It's not funny. I know. But sometimes I need to laugh. I watch a lot of comedies on television. I figure it'll make me feel better, but it doesn't. I want to laugh. I want to feel like it, but I can't. The thing is, I feel like I don't *deserve* to laugh. Because of what I did to you. Until you can get up and walk and talk and everything, then I feel like I shouldn't have a life. Not a real one.

That's guilt talking. I know it. The judge made me go to counselling.

I wasn't against it. Whatever works. She said I needed to come to terms with the consequences of what I did. See, she's not really into punishment. She doesn't want to see me in jail because she thinks that won't do me or society any good. Maybe she's right and maybe she's wrong. I don't know.

A lot of people think they know what's right and wrong. They think they know how the world works and how they fit into it. But I've noticed people like that, they don't really get it about life. All they know is one little slice of life, the slice that involves them. And they can be as sure of themselves as they want, and it isn't going to make any difference to the world because of them being sure of things. It's just a put-on. It's just a fake front that they put on to fool other people.

I'm not fooled. Not by anyone. That judge doesn't fool me. She thinks she's fixing the world, but she's just making herself feel good. That's okay. We all do that. How else do you get through life, huh?

[pauses]

So I've been going to counselling. If the court didn't make me, I wouldn't do it. I couldn't make myself get out of the apartment for it. But they track me. They've got tabs on me. They know what I'm doing and what I'm not doing.

Just like you. They got you monitored. Every time you take a breath they know it. Every time you blink, if you ever blink again, they'll know it. Not to mention all the other functions they got you on.

I heard you went home for a while. Must have been some logistical nightmare, moving you in your condition.

[pauses]

But the counsellor tries to make me see that guilt is not a productive thing. Guilt rarely helps anyone. Oh, really, doc? I didn't know that. I always thought guilt was the most useful thing anyone could haul around with them.

Yeah, I can be sarcastic when the situation demands it.

We talk about you. He asks me what being guilty will do for you. I tell him nothing. And then he spreads his hands, like he's saying, see, all your troubles can be over if you would just assimilate that.

So useful.

I get on his case because he has this attitude about truck drivers. A lot of people do. They think we're kind of dumb. It's true. You tell people you drive a truck for a living and they assume you don't know anything except big rigs and highways.

Well, there are dumb truck drivers. But there are dumb people everywhere. And we know what's going on in the world.

Take me, for example. I read. Not just crappy magazines but books. Real books. Classics. Like *The Arabian Nights* I was telling you about. I know what's going on in the world, too. Not just the world of the past, but today. Now. I read a newspaper every day. I read the local ones wherever I am, so I know a lot more about the world than someone who only reads their one local paper. I have a wider perspective, you know what I mean?

And people don't understand about trucks. We're about the most important part of the economy. Without trucks nothing happens. If you've got something in your possession, you can be damn sure that it was hauled in a truck at some point. Guarantee it. At some point in its existence it was in a truck. You take all the trucks off the road, and the next day you don't have food, clothing, building materials, medicine. You've got nothing. That's what trucks do for you. They give you all those things. They make everything in the world happen.

[pauses]

If you can think, you're probably thinking: so what? What is this guy talking to me about trucks for?

I've got to talk about something. Trucks is what I know.

[pauses]

Movement.

You ever think about that? Life is movement. You stay still long enough, you don't move yourself or others, then either you're dead or you should be dead.

That's not something I'm making up.

It's something a lot of people don't understand.

Like you.

You don't get it. You think you can go on living like this, not moving.

Are you dreaming?

Is that what's keeping you going?

I don't want you to die.

That would be the worst. They'd probably open up a new case against me if that happened. Then I'd be up for murder or something. I don't know. Did I murder you? Are you already dead?

[pauses]

Because, I have to tell you, pathetic as I am, I'm way more alive than you are.

[pauses]

You want to blame me?

Go ahead.

Blame me all you want. Tell me I'll go to hell and burn there for eternity. Sure. That would be better than what I've got going on with me now.

But I'll tell you something. I may have put you here, but you're the one who's keeping yourself here. I read about coma patients. They can wake up. There's people who wake up after years and years. You think they couldn't wake up before that? Sure they could. Why would twenty years make a difference? It wouldn't. They just didn't *want* to wake up earlier. Just like you don't *want* to.

Well fuck that.

You *need* to want to, okay?

You *need* to.

[pauses]

The nurses are here to look after your *needs.*

[pauses]

Okay. They're gone. They told me something. You want to hear it?

Your wife went into labor.

Yeah.

How about that, huh? Your kid is getting born. She's a girl, in case you care. Your wife told me. The nurse said she's down the hall right now, in the maternity ward. New life getting born there. Best part of the hospital, you know. Best thing that can happen is new life. Babies. They keep the world young.

You're going to have a brand new daughter and you don't care.

At least as far as I can tell.

[pauses]

After I finish talking to you I have to get a doctor to sign this form that I was here and then I have to report to the probation officer. Tell him I'm doing my sentence. What the court wants me to do.

[pauses]

Maybe your wife is right. Maybe we bonded when we crashed. It could be. Life is a mystery, right? No one knows what made us. No one knows where we're going.

She says you have an imagination. She says she's sure all kinds of things are happening in your brain, that you are swimming up through the murk and you are trying to find the surface. All she's doing is throwing you life preservers. Do you see them from where you are? Do you see the donuts floating on the water above you?

Because I sure don't. I want to, but all I see around me, when I bother to look, is darkness. It's like this black fog. I want to get out of it, but I can't.

Wish someone would throw me a life preserver. Anything.

Wish someone would kill me.

That'd be the best thing now, I think. You'd be done with me. Maybe if I killed myself, you'd be released.

Is that what you want?

You want me punished?

It's not a crazy thought. If I was in your position, I think I'd want me dead. That sense of justice, you know. It's a primitive thing, but it's real. It's what we're made of.

Like I said before, truck drivers can be a pretty fatalistic bunch. I thought about that accident a lot. Every day. Sometimes all day. Over and over. It's like this movie that plays in my brain. And it's stuck on a loop and it won't get out of it. I dream about it. In the dream I never veer away. You never veer away. We just go over the same sequence, just like it happened in real life.

Isn't that crazy? Doing the same thing. Like an obsession, where you can't deviate from the sequence by even the most insignificant detail.

And what I think, when it plays over in my mind, is one of us *should* have died.

Really.

It was a big enough event that one of us, if the laws of physics make any sense, should be done. Finished.

Now, what seems to have happened is that you took on that role, but you didn't go all the way. Not blaming you. Not saying you did or are doing anything wrong. Just saying that maybe our roles got messed up. Maybe fate had it that I was supposed to die, and things got mixed up, and you ended up being the one to die, but the fates, they knew something got mixed up so they didn't let you go all the way. Not quite. Because you know you're not the one.

I am.

I'm willing to reverse roles.

I'm willing to be that one.

If it means you'll come back.

Will it?

If I give myself the ultimate punishment, if I take myself out, will that balance the accounts? Then you can come back, be yourself. You won't have to be held like a watch in a pawn shop, waiting for your life to tick down, waiting for someone to come back for you and return you to life.

[pauses]

All I need is a sign. Something to tell me this is what you want. If you can hear anything, if you can hear the simplest sound, just acknowledge me. Just tell me that's what you want.

I could do it. Easily. I could do it right now. Find some pills to take. I'm in a hospital, should be easy to do. Or find a scalpel. Cut my wrists. All I would need is a minute or so in the bathroom. Even in a hospital, you cut yourself good enough and bleed out, there's nothing they can do for you. You'd be dead.

I'll do it. I'm ready.

Just give me the signal.

Give me the word.

We're twins, me and you. We collided our lives and now one of us has to go. Let it be me.

Don't let it be you.

I'm looking around this room right now for something to do the job. I'm ready, man. Ready to take myself out. Ready to meet my maker.

Just give me the word.

Anything.

Any.

Thing.

[a long pause]

[cries]

[a very long silence]

Oh, man. I didn't expect this.

[more cries]

[silence]

[wails, loud and sustained]

Here come the nurses again.

[pauses]

Did you hear that? Did you?

Oh, God.

[pauses]

That was your daughter bawling. Your daughter. They brought her to you. They wanted you to see her. To hear her.

Did you?

[pauses]

Oh, God. Oh, man. I don't believe it. I don't believe it. I don't believe it.

gary hawken

Uh. What's that noise?

    [pauses]

    [blinks]

    Where am I?

    [pauses]

    Who are you, little one? Where's your mother?

about the author

Mario Milosevic's books include the novels *Claypot Dreamstance*, *The Last Giant*, and *Terrastina and Mazolli*, and the poetry collections *Animal Life*, *Fantasy Life*, and *Love Life*. He lives in the Pacific Northwest.